Love in the Trenches

Corey Robinson

**Lock Down Publications and Ca$h
Presents**
Love in the Trenches
A Novel by *Corey Robinson*

Love in the Trenches

Lock Down Publications
Po Box 944
Stockbridge, Ga 30281

Visit our website @
www.lockdownpublications.com

Lock Down Publications
Like our page on Facebook: Lock Down Publications @
www.facebook.com/lockdownpublications.ldp
Book interior design by: **Shawn Walker**
Edited by: **Sunny Giovanni**

Corey Robinson

Stay Connected with Us!

Text **LOCKDOWN** to 22828 to stay up-to-date with new
releases, sneak peaks, contests and more…
Thank you.

Submission Guideline.

Submit the first three chapters of your completed manuscript to ldpsubmissions@gmail.com, subject line: Your book's title. The manuscript must be in a .doc file and sent as an attachment. Document should be in Times New Roman, double spaced and in size 12 font. Also, provide your synopsis and full contact information. If sending multiple submissions, they must each be in a separate email.

Have a story but no way to send it electronically? You can still submit to LDP/Ca$h Presents. Send in the first three chapters, written or typed, of your completed manuscript to:

LDP: Submissions Dept
Po Box 944
Stockbridge, Ga 30281

DO NOT send original manuscript. Must be a duplicate.

Provide your synopsis and a cover letter containing your full contact information.

Thanks for considering LDP and Ca$h Presents.

Corey Robinson

Chapter One

"Yeah, girl, Nahvi's ass been talking real crazy lately. He's saying he's ready to pull out of the streets and go legit, but little does he know, if he pulls through with his brilliant idea, I already got niggas lined up to take his spot. Bitch, I was born to be a baller wife, not some lame ass Stepford wife. Who in the hell does he think I am? Girl, if he believes that I'm going to stick around once that fast money stops coming in then he is dumber than I thought."

Janahvi Karter had come in from the block early and let himself into the plush condo that him and Monica shared. She had her long, smooth caramel-colored legs propped up on the arm of the couch, while she laid back with her head on one of the throw pillows. Her cell phone was glued tightly to her ear while she had a conversation with one of her grimy ass friends.

Nahvi couldn't believe what he had heard so he walked up on her and stared down angrily into her eyes. "You're lucky my ass ain't trying to go back to the pen, or you'd be swallowing a hollow tip right now."

Monica dropped her phone and jumped up from where she had laid as soon as Nahvi got the words out of his mouth. She had to think quickly enough to save face. "Oh my God, Nahvi. It's not how it sounded. I was just playing around and talking shit with my girl Tonya. I didn't mean anything I said. I swear."

Nahvi had been introduced to Monica by one of his cell mates while he was in the joint. They had somehow managed to build what he thought was the real thing. Getting to know each other through phone calls and letters wasn't enough for Nahvi's lonely heart, so six months into their relationship he sent her the money to move closer so they could do the visitation thing. When Monica came on her visit, she took his breath away. Not only was she thick in all the right places but she had the face of a supermodel. It seemed like she had her shit together and that was enough for Nahvi. Monica never missed a visit, and when he was released a year later, she was right there with open arms waiting to pick him up.

Nahvi had been sentenced to an eight-year bid for an assault charge that he had caught one night up in the club. He didn't know that the bitch he'd had grinding on his dick belonged to someone else, and when the nigga stepped to him Nahvi straightened that shit. Before he got booked he held mad respect in the streets. Some would have even considered him to be on kingpin status with plenty of money in his pockets and plenty of honeys on his nutsack. However, once he was out of sight, he was also out of mind. The niggas he used to roll with and the bitches who used to sweat him for a spot on his arm slowly forgot he existed. He tried hard not to let that shit get to him, but deep down, it still hurt him to his heart. It was only right before he was released that those who had neglected him started to come back around, but Nahvi dissed they ass. He didn't have room for fake ass muthafuckas in his life. Besides, he had Monica and he felt like she was all he needed.

He told himself that when he got out he would ball hard for two years just so he could stack more paper on top of what he already had stashed, and then he would leave the game for good. He thought he was ready to settle down and do things the legal way with someone who appreciated him, but leaving the streets behind would be harder than he expected. It was all he knew, and after he walked in on Monica's phone call it had him more fucked up than ever.

"Aye, Nahvi. Nigga, where ya' mind at? Your ass ain't said two words the whole time we been here. Shit, you ain't even felt on no ass or nothing. Something going on with you and Monica? Come on, man, you know you can talk to me." Meek asked while Nahvi sat there and stared out into the crowd of horny men as they put their hard-earned cash into the g-strings the strippers wore. He wondered how many of them had a wife and kids at home. And then he thought about Monica and all the ways he could kill her and get away with it.

Nahvi had hooked up with Ahmeek Johnson by word of the streets. Meek had come to town and made the trenches bleed cocaine and x-pills while Nahvi had been locked up. When Nahvi touched back down, Meek sent him a message to contact him when he was ready to get back on his grind. Nahvi waited a whole month because he didn't want to seem desperate. When he finally gave Meek a call, he passed him back the crown he had worn before he caught that case. He liked Meek's style off rip because although he had shit locked down, he wasn't no prideful or flashy nigga. He was more humble and down to earth and didn't mind sharing his good fame.

Nahvi looked at Meek sideways and replied in a cantankerous voice, "Man, fuck Monica. That bitch name tastes like shit in my mouth now."

Meek looked at him crazy because he had never heard him talk about Monica that way. Instead, he had always talked about her as if she would be the woman he'd spend forever with. "Man, I don't know why you let that bitch get to you. Forget about her ass. Shit, look at them fine ass women out there. Just pick you one out and lock that shit down."

"Nah, Meek, them hoes shaking they ass is played the fuck out. Besides, what I look like taking one of them home and talking about settling down? Do you know how many hands have been on that ass? Fuck all that. I wanna find me someone with some damn sense in they head. I need someone I can grow old with and maybe even plant some seeds in. I can't do that with none of them bitches. That fast shit ain't where it's at no more. I relinquished my player card when I got with Monica."

"Yeah, and look where the hell it got you. Right back here at the strip club looking at pussy prints. Come on, Nahvi, snap outta that shit. Hell, I never thought Monica was the right one for you anyway."

Nahvi seemed vexed by what Meek had said because he never knew that he felt that way. Meek had always been cool when Monica was around so Nahvi was curious as to why his boy made that comment. "I ain't never knew you felt that way but I'm curious as to what made you come to that conclusion. How you know what's right for me?"

Meek pursed his lips and shrugged before he answered, "Well, I know that I've only known you a little over a year but I can tell you that when you're with her it's almost as if something is missing. Your ass don't be content and you be looking all distant and shit. It's like you're irritated and can't wait to get away from her. I only respected her ass on the strength of you and I know this ain't what you wanna hear but Monica's ass got gold digger written all over it. Stop spending that gwop on her and see what happens."

"Well, that won't be a problem because I already took her key and told her to have her shit outta my space by the time I got back. Dawg, I walked in earlier and caught her on the phone with Tonya talking about leaving me if I got out of the game. I'm telling you, man, I just wish that I could find one woman who looked at me and not my street cred but I feel like there's not one who exists. I guess I'm gonna be alone forever."

"Don't worry, dawg, she'll come along one day. And when she does, you'll pick up on that shit instantly. In the meantime, I say we go over there and tap on some ass."

Meek stood but Nahvi chose to stay in his seat. He just wasn't feeling the same way his boy was. A female was the reason he was in such a stupor so he thought it would be best to keep his distance. "Nah, man, I think I'm gonna pass for now. You go ahead though. I'ma stay here and chill until you get back."

Nahvi sat back and watched while Meek went and did his thing. He sipped on his glass of Ciroc and laughed when he saw Meek walk up to one of the dancers and whisper something in her ear. When Meek turned and winked at him and then walked off with the woman, Nahvi knew it would be a minute before his friend returned so he ordered another drink and then sat back to think about his next move.

Before he could top off his next glass he looked up and saw Monica come through the entrance with a nigga from around the way named Jared glued to her side. He hadn't even left her more than two hours ago and she'd already clutched onto the next up and comer. He was truly disappointed in Monica and couldn't believe that he'd never saw the signs.

"Grimy ass bitch."

He decided to wait until they sat down and then he finished his drink and walked over to where they were at. Monica was so engrossed in the knot that Jared pulled out of his pocket that she didn't notice Nahvi until he was right up on them. He could tell that she wanted to get up and make a run for it but Jared had his arm around her so tight she couldn't move.

"Sup, Monica? You handle that shit?" Nahvi asked her while Jared sat there looking like a galoot.

"Oh, hey, Nahvi. You do know Jared, don't you?"

Jared smiled a crooked smile and nodded at Nahvi but he didn't return the gesture because his focus was solely on Monica.

"Aye, you get your shit outta my space like I told your ass to or not?"

Before she could answer, Jared stood and pointed his four-five right in Nahvi's face. "You better watch who the fuck you talking to, playa. This my bitch now so back the hell up with that shit before I back your ass up myself."

Nahvi had never been a pussy but he held his hands up in surrender. He was a convicted felon and the last thing he needed to do was get caught up in some gun play with a nothing ass nigga like Jared. He had come to the club clean because he didn't feel like he needed to be strapped. Drama was the last thing he expected to run into while he was there. "You got it, man, and you can have that bitch!" Nahvi exclaimed as he backed away slowly from them. He could feel his heart about to beat out of his chest because of the immense anger he felt inside. He wondered how she could have moved on so quickly and came to the conclusion that she must have already been in the nigga's arms before shit went sour between them. Nahvi knew there was no way he could stay up in that club and watch Monica's foul ass all night, so he sent Meek a quick text and told him he'd meet up with him later. He then quickly made his way to the exit but before he could walk out, he heard Monica's voice behind him.

"Nahvi, I really hope there's no hard feelings between us. Maybe we could at least still be friends."

He couldn't believe that she had fixed her mouth to say some shit like that to him. She had nerve to think that they could be anything after the cold way she had played him and after all that had happened. He no longer held any type of respect for her sanctimonious ass so he didn't waste his breath responding to her comment. Instead, he threw her deuces and turned around to walk out. He hopped in his ride but before he could get his key in the ignition his cell phone vibrated. When he saw that it was Meek he thought about not answering it but he wasn't the one he was beefing with so he pushed the call button. "Sup, Meek? You get my message, nigga?"

"Yeah, man, you good? What the hell you leaving for? Did something happen?" Meek asked him in a concerned voice.

"Yeah, I'm straight. Just got too much shit on my mind. I'm about to go to the crib and chill. Catch up with me tomorrow so we can go over the details of that ride we need to make."

"Aight, tomorrow then. I'm about to lay this pipe down. Peace out, my brotha!"

When Meek hung up, Nahvi turned off his cell phone. He just wasn't in the mood to be bothered anymore. He thought about the plans they had made for the weekend and he couldn't wait to get away. A small-time dealer out of Austell needed five bricks of re-up and although Nahvi usually didn't leave town for such a small amount he knew that he needed the distance from all the bullshit going on with Monica. He knew it would do him some good and help him clear his head. He and Meek had the trip planned for the weekend but there were still a few kinks for them to work out to ensure that everything went as planned.

The shit Nahvi had going on with Monica had him fucked up in the head. He really thought that she was his soulmate but was glad that he found out the truth sooner than later. He was also glad that he'd never told her about the safe he had hidden in the closet floor because she turned out to be just another snake and he was sure she would have taken him for all he had. Before Nahvi pulled out of the parking lot he reached in his console and pulled out the small red box he'd picked up from Tiffany's. He lifted the top and stared at the six-carat diamond that was perched on a platinum band. He had planned to propose to Monica within the next week. "Guess I won't be needing this anymore."

He closed the box and put it back where he got it from, telling himself that he would return it the first chance he got. He just couldn't believe that he had been so blind to her motives. He had always been smarter than that when it came to women but somewhere along the way he lost his focus.

When he made it home and walked into his condo he could tell right away what a difference not having Monica there made. It was eerily quiet and although he should have enjoyed the peace it was something he didn't want to get used to. He liked having someone to come home to after a long stressful night in the streets with the fellas. He just couldn't understand why Monica didn't keep it real with him. He was good to her and gave her anything she could have ever wanted. He thought she was happy with him, but it turned out that happiness wasn't enough. Nahvi decided not to sit around and wallow in his sorrows all night so he went and took a shower and then fell fast asleep on the couch.

The next morning he was awakened by loud knocking coming from his front door. He had thought about not answering it but remembered that Meek was supposed to stop by so they could finalize their trip to Austell. He got his ass up and answered the door only to find that it wasn't Meek on the other side.

"I'm so sorry, Nahvi. Would you please let me have one more chance? I'll never fuck up again. Please. I know we can work this out."

He couldn't believe that Monica had the nerve to show up at his door and think that shit could smell sweet between them. She really did think that he was a dumb ass nigga but he would show her once and for all that he was smarter than she thought. He gave her a nefarious look and exclaimed, "Hell no, you ain't getting another chance! The fuck is you thinking? What happened to that nigga you had in your clutches last night?"

"His wife, that's what happened. Please, Nahvi, I know I fucked up but just give me a chance to make things right. You know I don't have anywhere else to go."

Nahvi stood and stared at her for a minute and the thought of giving her another chance actually crossed his mind. He reminisced on all the good times they had shared and realized that they outweighed the bad. However, he knew that if he let her get away with snaking him once, she'd just turn around and do it again. She looked at him through pleading eyes and waited for his answer, but before he could get the words out, Meek walked up and looked at Monica sideways before he stepped into the apartment.

Monica crossed her arms over her chest and had nerve to have an attitude. Those little temper tantrums used to turn Nahvi on but that shit had played out. "Well, are you going to let me come back home or not? You know you gonna miss this kitty kat."

Nahvi gave her a mannish smile and then slammed the door in her face. He needed Monica to realize that he wasn't no soft ass nigga that she could do any kind of way and he damn sure wasn't pussy-whipped. He'd been deep inside some of the best and knew that there was plenty more out waiting to wet his dick up.

"You're a piece of shit, Janahvi Karter, and you will get yours. I promise you that."

He walked away from the door and ignored the slurs that Monica spat at him. Her threats didn't mean shit because he felt like she'd gotten just what she deserved. He went back in the living where Meek waited so they could work out the details for their run. Little did he know, the ride would be more than worth it.

Chapter Two

"Attention, ladies and gentlemen. The park will be closing in fifteen minutes. Please use this time to make your way safely to the exit and, as always, we hope you experienced the joy of a lifetime here at Six Flags over Georgia. We look forward to seeing you again soon. Have a nice night."

The announcer's voice broke Ashley from the trance that she had fell in and caused her to blink rapidly against the bright lights. Once she had been brought back to reality, Tracey's voice was the first thing she noticed.

"Ashley, damn, girl. Where the hell is your mind at? I've done called your name like three times."

Tracey and Ashley had been friends since the third grade and had planned the trip to Six Flags ever since their high school graduation. However, their lives got in the way and they went in opposite directions, but when they reconnected they were finally able to pull it off.

Ashley let out a delicate sigh before she answered, "Girl, my focus was on that fine specimen over there by the snack booth."

Tracey looked to where she pointed at and then unhooked her seat strap. She proceeded to get off the ride before she commented on the man Ashley pointed to. "Uh-uh, girl, you should be tired of dealing with men. Besides, he looks like just another street thug. If you need a man that bad, I can hook you right on up. David has plenty of single friends that would be perfect for you."

Ashley gave her a bewildered look and replied, "Hell, no! You always try to hook me up with those lame ass white boys and you know that vanilla is not my flavor, so I think I'll pass."

David and Tracey had been together since middle school, and as far as she knew, he had always been faithful to her. He was really cool for a white dude, and him and Tracey were perfect for each other. However, Ashley had been attracted to her own race. There was just something about the dark brown pigment of a brother's skin that turned her on. She had tried to date white before but she just couldn't feel their rhythm. It was the most uncomfortable thing she had experienced. She felt like their kisses were too wet, their head game was sloppy and their groove in the bedroom was boring as hell. She craved that hard yet oh so soft vibe that only a thug from the trenches could give her. She had been unlucky in the relationship department and had recently broken up with her ex after coming in one day and finding him with another woman. She knew that she shouldn't have been thinking about another man but there was just something about the one she saw and she couldn't pull her eyes away from him.

She was aching to get a closer look, so she got off the ride and stepped a little closer to where he stood. She allowed her gaze to start at his Nike adorned feet, and if what they say about a man's shoe size was true, she would be in for a nice surprise. His black heavily starched RocAWear jeans hung respectfully just below his waist. Her eyes traveled up a little further to the outline of his muscles and wished that she could replace the white Nike t-shirt that hugged them so tightly. The diamond encrusted Rolex that adorned his wrist gave his smooth, dark brown skin a bright glow. His hair was neatly trimmed and edged into a Caesar cut with waves so deep it made her suddenly want to go surfing. His arms were covered in tattoos that surely told his life story and she imagined herself lying back and reading every single page. His face was handsome although his look was hard as if he were challenging someone.

His sensual lips outlined by a sharply cut goatee made her blush at the thought of what they could do to her body.

"Sup, Shawty?" The stranger asked before Ashley even realized he was up on her. His voice was strong but smooth at the same time and she could feel the butterflies in her stomach escape from their cocoons and flutter with life. He had already touched something inside of her and yet, he hadn't touched her at all.

"Um. Hi. Hello," was embarrassingly all she could manage to say before Tracey chimed in and spoiled the mood.

"Uh-uh. Come on, Ash. We gotta get the hell out of here so let's go before you or him get any crazy ideas." She placed a hand softly around Ashley's wrist to pull her away but it was as if her friend's feet were stuck in cement and couldn't move.

Suddenly, the dark, handsome stranger looked at Tracey and spoke up. "Aye, man. Come on and just chill for a minute. Let me holla at ya girl real quick. I ain't gonna bring her no harm."

Instead of loosening her grip, Tracey tightened it and Ashley knew that her small wrist would be sore and bruised by the time she could get it out of her friend's grasp.

"My name is not Ma and I think my girl is good. She don't need any more associates in her life. So, see ya!"

Ashley finally pulled herself from the hold and spoke up. "Thanks, Trace, but I think I'm old enough to speak for myself."

Tracey huffed and stormed away with an attitude in the direction of the exit and left Ashley alone with the stranger.

He let out a small chuckle and held his hand out for Ashley to shake. "JaNahvi Karter. But everyone just calls me Nahvi." He spoke every syllable perfectly as if he had rehearsed it.

Ashley wondered how many other women he had said it to. She couldn't allow another man to come into her life with ill intentions no matter how fine they were. "Ashley Taylor. Nice to meet you," she stated with a red face and reached her hand out to meet his.

However, instead of shaking it he pulled it to his lips and kissed the back of it. The gesture made her feel as if her knees would buckle under her. She felt like the man in front of her was the perfect gentleman except for one issue. He had dope boy written all over him, and while he held on to her small hand firmly, she tried to push the thought out of her mind.

Her ex had been a dope boy and was really heavy in the streets. All the ones she had ever came across had the same reputation. They were known to be liars and cheaters and tricked off the same product they sold. Women flocked to them because of their status and they ate that shit up. Ashley never could understand why they couldn't settle down with one woman. For some reason, they felt the need to have a side piece and she refused to be put in that position again. She had been with Kelvin for over two years when she found out that he'd fathered two children with two different women all while he was with her. She really cared about him and wanted things to work out between them, so she forgave his misdeeds. But when she walked in that day and caught him deep in another woman on the same bed he gave it to her in, she was finished and had sworn off men for good. It had been months since that incident happened and Ashley was still single. Her broken heart made it difficult for her to move on.

She pulled her hand from Nahvi's soft touch and looked up at him. "Hey, it was nice meeting you, but I have to go find my girl before she leaves my ass. Have a good night."

When she turned to walk away, his voice intervened and held her captive. "Can I at least get your number? Maybe we could hang out and chill sometime."

She was hesitant at first but when he licked his lips like LL Cool J did in that *I Need Love* video, there was no way she could refuse him. He pulled out his phone and handed it to her. She quickly programmed her number before she changed her mind and handed it back to him. When she was finally able to walk away she could still feel his closeness. She turned her head and saw that he followed behind her. She raised her eyebrows as if questioning his motive.

He smiled a toothy smile and stated, "Just making sure you get to your ride safely."

Ashley smiled back at him and then looked up and down his six-foot frame. "Alright, I guess you can do that much since Tracey did leave me hanging."

While they walked slowly side by side to the parking lot, neither one of them said a word. It was as if they had left each other with nothing to say but in a good sense. Ashley had the burning desire to ask him what he did for a living, but she wasn't really sure she wanted to know the answer. She wondered how she would feel if she found out that he was just another corner boy. Would it even make a difference? She knew that she had just met him, but she was already feeling his vibe.

As soon as they walked out of the exit, Ashley notice Tracey as she stood by her car with hands on her hips. She looked like an angry yet worried mother who had just caught her daughter sneaking in the window after a long night out.

"Whoa, she don't look too happy about you and me walking out together. What's up with her anyway?" Nahvi asked curiously.

"She just doesn't want to see me get hurt again, that's all. She's just being a real friend."

"Yeah, I can't get mad at that, but she has nothing to worry about. I'm a gentleman and have no intentions of breaking anyone's heart. You're in good hands, ma."

"And how could I be so sure of that? I just met you, so I don't know what you're capable of."

"How 'bout you get to know me and then you can see for yourself. Let me take you out sometime."

Nahvi's voice was intoxicating and she could feel herself getting high off of his words. She thought about what he said for a second as the cool Georgia breeze blew across her face and pushed away some of the heat that Nahvi had made her feel. "I'll think about it and let you know when you call. Is that fair enough?"

"Hey, at least you didn't say no," he exclaimed and pulled her hand to his lips, kissing it one more time.

The gentleness of his touch brought a tingling sensation to her most sacred spot. All the signs her body gave her told her that she was in trouble but she completely ignored them. She pulled her hand from his and walked away quickly because if she would have stood there any longer, she may have let him have more than just her hand and that could have been dangerous. Ashley smiled at Tracey when she walked past her and got in the car. She didn't say one word to her because honestly, she couldn't. JaNahvi Karter had left her utterly speechless.

Chapter Three

Nahvi was still in a daze when he heard Meek's voice. "Damn, man. Where the hell you been at? I been looking for your ass everywhere."

Nahvi wanted to tell him that his mind had been on Ashley Taylor ever since she got in that car with her friend and rode away. He knew that he probably shouldn't have been entertaining thoughts of another woman, especially after the bullshit that Monica had put him through, but there was something about the one he had met that he just couldn't ignore. He had only ever dated women of his own race because he truly adored his black queens. However, after meeting Ashley it made him want to taste a different flavor. Maybe having a different kind of spice in his life would do him some good. Nahvi thought that maybe things could turn around for him after all. He was only a thug when he was out in the streets but behind closed doors and with his lady he liked to be a gentleman. Only a true lady could appreciate a man like him, something that Monica never did.

"Meek, my nigga. You wouldn't even believe my luck, man. I just met the most amazing woman."

"Ah, come on, Nahvi. How the hell you know you met someone amazing? How long did you actually spend with her? What, ten minutes? There's no way it could have been any longer than that, so how your ass know all that in such a short amount of time?"

"Now, Meek, ain't you the muthafucka that told me I would know as soon as I met the one? Well, dammit I'm telling you I met the one, so miss me with that bullshit you talking."

Meek shook his head and walked to the rental they had gotten for the trip. They had agreed to never take their own rides on run out of town just in case shit went sour on a deal. The last thing they needed was some out-of-town niggas putting look outs on their vehicles and coming for them. As soon as Nahvi got in the ride, Meek spoke up and tried to smooth things over with his boy.

"Aye, Nahvi, I'm sorry, man. I don't mean to be a sarcastic asshole or anything like that, but I just don't wanna see you get caught up with the wrong one again. You like a brother to me, dawg, and I just want what's best for you. All I'm saying is don't rush into something else. That's it. Aiight."

"Aiight, Meek. I know you have my best interest at heart and I ain't mean to lash out on you, but I'm telling you, as soon as she spoke I felt something inside of me shift. I ain't neva felt anything like that before. She could really be the one for me."

"You said the same shit about Monica and look what her flaw ass did to you, man. All that time and money you invested into that relationship was all for nothing. Your ass better be glad you ain't never get her pregnant. You'd have never been able to get rid of her ass then."

The two friends shared a laugh and then Meek started the car. He pulled out of the amusement park so they could make their way back home. Nahvi sat in the passenger seat quiet as he thought about Ashley. He hoped he didn't sound desperate, but he couldn't wait to hear her voice again. He leaned his seat back and closed his eyes while Meek pushed the gas pedal. Nahvi decided that as soon as he got in and settled, he would give Ashley a call. She had stirred up something inside of him and he couldn't contain it. His only hope was that she didn't turn out to be just another sack chaser.

Chapter Four

"Tracey, I am so glad that we finally went to Six Flags. Girl, I remember when we had planned it. Those were the good ole days when we were still young and innocent and free from bullshit. Now look at us, grown up with more drama than a soap opera." Ashley couldn't help but laugh at the comment she had made.

She started to get out of Tracey's car, but her friend's words stopped her. "Ash, look, girl. You know that I'm only hard on you about men because I care about you. I mean, come on. You're my best friend and I'm so tired of seeing you give your all to a man only for them to turn around and hurt you. I just want you to take your time. The right man will come along and sweep you off your feet and I'm sorry if I sound blessed, but I don't think you're going to find Mr. Right in the trenches."

"Tracey, I know that you care about what happens to me but you gotta let me find my own way. I appreciate your concern, I really, do but what's meant to happen is going to happen regardless of what you say. I'll be okay. Besides, I made a vow to myself not to give up the goodies until someone puts a ring on it."

"Yeah, right, bitch. You know that you are going to want some dick before then. Hell, you probably itching for some as we speak and that's okay but you gotta be like they are. Get that orgasm and keep it moving. You got to learn to keep your emotions in check so your soft ass don't catch not feelings."

Ashley rolled her eyes and asked with a smile, "And since when did you become such an expert, Miss I Been With My Man Since Middle School?"

Ashley knew that Tracey was right, but it was hard for her to keep her feelings from getting involved when she was intimate with a man. She had always been a very emotional person and because she had wanted to be loved so bad, she often confused for the moment with forever. She knew that she had a problem with trusting too quickly and too easily but the thought of living her fairytale blinded her sense. She grabbed her bag out of the backseat and before she shut the door, she tried to ease her friend's mind.

"Look, Trace, I'll work on keeping my emotions in check but I can't make any promises because I've been this way all my life. I let my heart lead me and it's kind of hard to change that up. I know you care about me and I love you for that. Now take your ass home to David."

"Yeah, 'cause I'm sure he's waiting up on me like I'm his child or something. I'll catch up with you later."

Tracey put her car in reverse and backed out of the parking spot as Ashley made her way upstairs. She pulled out her keys to open the door but before she got the key in the lock, her cell phone buzzed. Tracey had just left so she wondered who could be calling her. When she saw JaNavi's name light up on her screen she dropped everything she had in her arms and answered it. "Hello, Nahvi. I didn't expect to hear from you so soon. What a nice surprise."

His response made her blush like a young teenage girl with her first crush. "Well, I'm not sure how you thought I could have waited to call someone so beautiful. I couldn't afford to let too much time pass and risk someone else stealing my pot of gold."

"Pot of gold? Yeah right. Boy, don't no one else want me, and flattery will get you nowhere because it all sounds like bullshit to me and I can assure you that I've had plenty of it in my life." She turned her back to the door and slid down it because after she heard his voice, she no longer had the strength to keep standing.

"I'm not trying to bring any bullshit into your life. Actually, if you'll just give me a chance, I'd like to try and clean it up."

Ashley smiled at his response because she wanted so much to believe him and all he said. However, she knew better because she didn't know anything about him. He seemed like a good dude, but Ashley had always been a bad judge of character.

She thought for a second and then responded to what he said. "And how exactly do you plan on cleaning up the shit piles that others have left behind? What makes you different than anyone else?" Her ex-boyfriend Kelvin had run the same game on her and now her ass was sitting there with no one to come home to.

"Why don't you let me come scoop you and take you out for a night cap? I don't mind driving back to Austell to get you. You're definitely worth the trip."

"Well, you can drive back to Austell all you want but you're not going to find me there. I live in Atlanta."

He surprised her with his next words. "Well ain't that a coincidence because I live in Atlanta, too. I knew it was meant for us to meet. Now, tell me how to get to you."

Ashley couldn't believe that her and Nahvi lived in the same city but was thrilled at the revelation. Her mind told her to slow down but her heart was moving at full speed. "Alright, I'm a little tired from the ride back but I could probably hang for a couple of more hours." She gave Nahvi her address and hung up with a smile still plastered on her face. When she realized that she was still sitting outside the door of her apartment, she jumped up and went inside so she could prepare herself for whatever JaNahvi Karter had in store for her.

Corey Robinson

Chapter Five

Nahvi had never felt so excited in his life and after talking with Ashley, and finding out that they lived in the same city made shit even better. He took a quick shower with his Axe body wash and brushed his deep waves. He didn't want to overdo it so he put on some navy blue Sean John jeans with a white Sean John pull over. His white suede Timberlands made his outfit complete. He wasn't trying to rock too much jewelry, so he hooked a platinum diamond cut Cuban link around his neck and a navy blue banded Rolex around his wrist. He opened up his safe and pulled out a band of hundred-dollar bills. Ashley didn't seem like the type of chick that watched a nigga's wallet but he wanted to make sure he had enough ends in his pocket to spoil her, just in case. He looked at himself one last time in the mirror and headed for the door, only to be greeted by drama.

"Oh, hell no. Where you going this late looking all fresh and shit? And it better not be out with another bitch."

He let out an agitated sigh as soon as he heard Monica's voice. Leave it to her to fuck up a wet dream. "Monica, what the hell are you doing at my door? Shouldn't you be with one of those niggas you had lined up to take my spot instead of here fucking with me?"

"Now, Nahvi, I know that I was talking a lot of bullshit, but you know there ain't a nigga on earth that could fill me up like you do. I miss you and I was hoping that you'd let me come home. Don't I deserve another chance?" She pleaded with fake tears in the wells of her eyes, however, those tears didn't mean shit to Nahvi anymore. The feelings he held for her were stepped on as soon as he saw her on Jared's arm.

"Hell no, you know your ass don't deserve no second chance. Do you really think I'd take your grimy ass back after all that shit you was talking with Tonya, and then you in the strip club on another nigga's nut sack only a few hours later? Bitch, I need a woman who is going to have my back, even when I'm lying on it. Now get the hell outta my way. I got a real woman to go pick up."

He lightly pushed her to the side so he could get past and began to walk, away but not before Monica reached out and grabbed his arm to try and stop him. "A real woman? Nigga, you was all up in this pussy less than a week ago, talking about how much you love me and now you call yourself moving on that quick."

Nahvi pulled his arm away and gave her the look of death. He didn't owe Monica any type of explanation for what he was about to do. She'd had her chance with him but chose to fuck it up. "Please don't test me, Monica. You only know one side of me, and I can assure you that you don't want to meet the other one."

"Is that supposed to be some kind of threat, because I am not scared of your ass."

"I don't want you to be scared. I want you to be careful. Now excuse me, my woman is waiting." He walked away and left her standing there looking dumbfounded. He had never been the type of nigga to go backwards, nor did he hold on to baggage. Life was too short to let a bitch like Monica hold him back. She had taken him for granted long enough and it was time to move on. "Simple minded ass bitch."

Nahvi got in his Denali to go pick up Ashley, but before his key turned in the ignition, his cell buzzed. He saw that it was Meek. It was like he had a radar and knew when Nahvi was about to make a move. It couldn't have been business because that had already been taken care of so Nahvi sent his ass to voicemail. The only thing he wanted to focus on was the pretty ass white girl he was on his way to pick up. He put his foot on the gas pedal and rushed to get his Cinderella.

He began to feel nervous when he pulled into her complex. That feeling was new to him because he'd never been nervous about anything in his life. He had the bullshit with Monica going on and knew that he shouldn't have been bringing someone into it. He already knew how Monica got down and would show out if she ever saw him and Ashley out together, but he decided to cross that bridge when he got to it. He had already wasted almost three years of his life on her ass and refused to waste anymore. Nahvi wanted to get out of the dope game but he needed a woman who would look past all the riches it brought him and support his decision. He needed someone who was willing to stand by him even when it was all gone. He hoped that Ashley would be that one. There was just something about her that made him feel complete.

He finally got out of his ride and walked up the stairs that led to her apartment, but before he could raise his fist to knock, the door opened.

"Hello, Nahvi. I thought that it was a little too soon to invite you inside so I decided it would be best to meet you at the door. I hope you're okay with that."

The move she had made threw Nahvi completely off his game, but he was willing to look past it as long as she was comfortable. He was so used to women throwing themselves at him and it made him feel as if he were losing his touch. "Nah, you good. I completely understand where you coming from, and as long as you cool, I'm cool. Now let's get out of here because my black ass is hungry as hell."

Ashley laughed at his comment and then turned around to lock her door. While she had her back to Nahvi, he decided it would be a good time to check her out, and although her ass wasn't as fat as the women he had been used to, it was still nice and plump and looked good and juicy in her J-Lo jeans. When she turned around and shook her head, Nahvi knew that he had been busted.

"Well? Is it enough, or are you used to something bigger?"

Her question caught him off guard, but he answered it anyway. "Nah, ma. I ain't got no complaints."

They shared a quick laugh which told Nahvi that he'd found a woman with a sense of humor. Which he appreciated a lot. All the other women he'd encountered were so stuck on themselves that they rarely shared moments like the one him and Ashley had done. He opened the door to his ride for her when they got to his vehicle, a gesture his momma told him to always extend to a woman. She said that it would show them the respect he held, and to that day, he followed through.

"Thanks, Nahvi. I've never had a man open my door before. I always thought that maybe it was against thug policy or something."

"Well then, I guess you ain't never had a real thug in your life before, but I'm here to change your whole outlook on a lot of things. That is, if you let me."

Ashley didn't respond to the comment so Nahvi shut her door and then walked around to his. As soon as he got in, she put a hand on his arm and expressed how she really felt. "Look, Nahvi, I just got out of a really bad relationship less than six months ago, so if it seems like I'm a little hesitant at times, please don't take it personal."

He could only respect her honesty and figured that it would be best if he shared his own truth. "Well, it looks like we have something else in common because I just got out of one, too. However, mine was less than two weeks ago. Hope that doesn't bother you."

"Whoa, I guess you didn't waste any time getting back on your feet, but I'm cool with that as long as you don't bring me no drama. That's all I ask. Okay?"

"Okay, sounds like we have a deal."

However, Nahvi knew that he had just told Ashley his first lie because there was no way in hell that Monica was going to sit back and let him be happy with another woman. He decided to deal with it once the bullshit landed in his lap. He just didn't know that it would land sooner than later.

Corey Robinson

Chapter Six

"Oh, hell no. I know this niggas is not trying me with a fucking cracker bitch. Do you see that shit, Tonya?"

Tonya looked in the direction that Monica had pointed in and gaped her mouth open wide in surprise when she saw Nahvi and a white girl sitting in the booth of the Waffle House. The white girl seemed familiar but Tonya couldn't place her. She chalked it up to the fact that all white people looked alike. "Dayum, Moni, he didn't only move on to a different woman, he went to a completely different race. I know you gonna go in there and straighten his ass, right?"

Monica took a big gulp from her Hennessy and threw the empty red solo cup on Tonya's back floorboard. They had decided to hang out that night and possibly hook a baller but the block seemed to be moving slow so they poured them a drink and sat back hoping the niggas would show up soon. Monica had been checking her makeup in the mirror that was attached to the visor when she peeped Nahvi's money green Denali. She took a closer look and that was when she saw him and the white girl as they sat there laughing and looking like a real couple.

They seemed to be having a good time and it reminded Monica of the days when they first started out in their relationship. She knew that the fallout between them had been her fault, but she never would have guessed that he would one day want to get out of the dope game. She had only hooked up with Nahvi by the advice of her cousin who was serving a life sentence.

Nahvi just happened to live on the same cell block as he did and at Forest. Monica wanted to turn him down because a nigga in the pen did not appeal to her. What the hell could a man locked up give to her? However, when her cousin explained the power that Nahvi held in the streets she jumped on board quickly. She enjoyed having all that gwop spent on her and not to mention all the good dick that Nahvi gave to her just right, but when he started talking about getting out of the game, that shit turned her completely off.

There was no way that Monica could see herself lying beside a nine to five nigga at night. Just the thought of it made her sick to her stomach. How was he going to keep her hair and her nails done, and not to mention keep up with her designer wardrobe? Wasn't no legit nigga alive that would be able to keep up with that lifestyle. She was willing to work things out with Nahvi but planned to keep her a side nigga to stay in place for all her needs.

"Come on, Tonya, let's go in there and beat that white bitch ass about my motherfucking man." When she opened the car door and stepped out, she noticed that Tonya hadn't budged, so she walked around to the driver side and yanked her door open. "Come on, girl. What in the hell are you waiting on?"

Tonya grabbed the door and pulled it back closed. She rolled down the window and gave Monica a crazy look and told her what she didn't want to hear. "Girl, I am not about to go in there and confront nobody's ass. Do you not know that niggas reputation? Besides, that ain't my business anyway so you on your own with that one. I'll be sitting right here waiting for you to come back."

"Oh, so you just gonna let me run up in there all by myself?"

"Hell yeah. Bitch. Nahvi ain't did shit to me and he ain't did shit to you either. It's your own damn fault that he's in there entertaining the next bitch. He don't owe you nothing."

Monica placed her hands on her hips and said to the only friend she had, "You know what, Tonya? Fuck you. I thought that we were supposed to have each other's backs, but I see now that your scary ass ain't on board." When Tonya didn't respond to her antic, Monica turned around and stormed off. She was on a mission to go in and get her man back.

When Monica walked in the restaurant, she could tell from the look on the white girl's face that she knew she was coming for her. The pep in her step and the click of her heels announced her presence before she even got to the table where they sat at, but somehow, she still managed to catch Nahvi off guard.

"Who in the hell is this white bitch, Nahvi?"

He shook his head from embarrassment and then held it down in the palms of his hands before he finally looked up and responded. "Monica, why in the hell are you in here fucking with me right now?"

"I wanna know who in the hell you think you are, being in here with the next bitch. Especially a fucking cracker bitch. How could you just move on so quickly like what we had didn't mean shit to you?"

Ashley began to grab her things and pulled out her cell phone like she had an important call to make. Monica believed that white people were known to call the police on black folks, so she needed to know just who Ashley was dialing.

"Bitch, is you calling the police on me?"

Ashley ignored her and spoke into the phone, "Hey, Tracey, I know it's late but I really need you to come pick me up."

Monica didn't know who Tracey was, but she decided that if the bitch showed up and wanted some, she had plenty of whoop ass to go around. Nahvi ignored her and focused his attention back on the woman he was there with. Monica became even angrier when he reached out and grabbed one of the girl's hands, and said in a soft voice that she had never heard him use before, "Call Tracey back and tell her never mind. I'll take you home, Ashley."

"No, I think I'll pass. You assured me that there would be no drama and yet, it shows up on the first date." Ashley looked up at Monica when she said it so that she would know it was her she was talking about, and that set her off even more.

"Drama? Bitch, you saying I brought you drama? You ain't seen none like you gonna see if you don't stay the hell away from my man." Monica spat with much attitude.

Nahvi finally cut in and gave her the business. "I am not your man, Monica. Remember, you had niggas lined up to take my spot, so why the hell are you still lurking around fucking with me?" He stood up from his seat and got right in her face to spit his next words, "You about to make the beast come out of me, so if you don't wanna feel my wrath, I suggest you walk your dumb ass right back out the way you came in."

Monica felt the chills as they crept up on her skin and decided that she better take heed to what Nahvi had said. She had heard war stories about him and the reputation he had before he went to prison, so she knew that he was ruthless and not to be fucked with. She felt like she had got her point across, so she looked at the white bitch one more time and walked out. Monica knew that pussy was a man's weakness, and after the show she had put on, she knew Nahvi wouldn't be getting any from the snowflake, so she planned to go back to the condo they used to share and convince him to give her some dick. She was going to fuck him so good that he would never think about another woman again. But what she didn't know was that Nahvi was stronger than she thought.

Chapter Seven

Nahvi was pissed at Monica for what she had done. He still couldn't get over the fact that she came into the restaurant and fucked up his and Ashley's vibe like that. He didn't understand how she could have possibly thought that confronting him would win her some favor. He was thankful when she finally left and tried to smooth things over with Ashley. However, things didn't go as planned.

"Ashley, come on. I never would have expected Monica to show up and show out like that. It's not even like her to do some shit that foul, but I guess I didn't know her like I thought I did. Please stay and let's finish our evening. Don't let a simple bitch like that ruin what we got going on. Come on, we had a good vibe in there."

He could tell from the look in her eyes that his pleas went unheard, but he refused to give up that easy. Ashley stood with her arms crossed over her chest and breathed heavily while she waited for her friend to show up and rescue her. Nahvi knew that he didn't have long so he took advantage of every second.

"Look, Monica is just a woman acting like she's been scorned, but she did that shit to herself. I'm a good nigga, Ashley, and all I'm asking for is the chance to show you. Don't let that bitch steal your joy. I mean, come on and be honest, you were having a good time. You never even stopped smiling once; just think about it. I could make you smile like that for the rest of your life, but you gotta be willing to let me."

She finally spoke and although it wasn't what he wanted to hear, it was enough to satisfy him. "Nahvi, yes, I did have a wonderful time with you, but I don't do drama too well and trust me, I know how black women get down when it comes to their men. Like you. I mean, I really, really like you but shit like that is not something I'm willing to put up with for any amount of happiness. So, I'll tell you what, you get rid of her for good and then give me a call. Until then, lose my number."

Before she could get another word out her ride pulled up in the parking lot and Tracey didn't waste any time stating how she felt. "Come on, Ash, get in the car. I tried to tell you to leave them trench boys alone. Maybe now you'll listen to me."

Once Ashley got in the car, Tracey sped out of the parking lot and left Nahvi standing there wondering how in the hell he was going to fix what had happened. He was going to make Monica pay for what she had done. The buzzing of his cell phone pulled him from his thoughts and when Nahvi saw that it was Meek, he answered.

"Sup, Meek? Nigga, ain't you calling me kinda late? Something up I need to know about?"

"Aye, man, I hope I'm not disturbing you, but I got a call from that Austell nigga and he say he got a homie interested in making some investments. Says we could drop back by tomorrow and meet up, but I'm gonna let you make the call on this one."

Nahvi didn't like the sound of what Meek had said because it had him wondering why the cat didn't mention his homie while they were there. It felt to him like something was off, so he shared his feelings with Meek. "Nigga, that shit don't sound kinda shady to you? Why did he wait for us to get all the way back home and then set something like that up?"

"I don't know, dawg, but from what he say, it's a lot of paper on the line."

"Yeah, and all money ain't good money, my boy. I say we pass on this one. Shit just don't sound right. You cool with that?"

Meek agreed with him although Nahvi could tell that wasn't really what he wanted to do. "I'm cool with whatever you say. You know I'd never go against your word because to me, your word is bond."

Nahvi liked the fact that Meek never went against him. He had been more loyal than any nigga he'd ever fucked with and he knew that he could trust Meek with his life. He stood with his phone stuck to his ear but was without words, so he couldn't blame his boy for wondering what was up.

"Nahvi, nigga you mighty quiet. You alright?"

Nahvi told him the truth. "Man, Meek, I was out with the chick I'd met at the park and Monica's dumb ass showed up and showed the fuck out."

"Damn, how you hook up with ol' girl so fast?"

"Well, it turns out that she lives right here in the A-T-L. Told you she's the one. Shit ain't just a coincidence. This shit was meant to be, my boy!" Nahvi exclaimed excitedly.

"Okay, and it seems like your ass got it bad already. But what happened after Monica showed her ass?"

"Man, Ashely ain't like that shit so she called her friend to come pick her up, and then told me to lose her number until I took care of my drama with Monica. Shits just crazy, man, and my ass don't know what to do."

"I'll tell you what to do. Put that foot in Monica's ass and put her in her place. You got to show that bitch that it's really over between y'all. Ain't no other way to tell her."

"Dawg, my momma would roll over in her grave if I put my hands on a woman. She raised me better than that."

Nahvi had lost his mother when he was fourteen years old at the hands of the man she thought she would spend the rest of her life with. When he started putting his hands on her, she realized that she had made a mistake, but it was too late to leave him. Nahvi had tried many times to intervene but he was just too weak to stand up against the man's strength. One day, he beat her so badly she never recovered and eventually succumbed to her injuries, changing the course of Nahvi's life forever. The man was still in the pen paying for the life he took twenty years ago.

"I feel what you saying because my old girl taught me the same shit, but unlike you, I don't always listen to the advice I'm given. Sometimes you gotta go against everything you were told and put a bitch in they place. It's the only way."

"Yeah, I hear you talking, but look, I gotta cut this call short because my black ass is tired as hell. I'm bout to go home and crash. I'll get up with you tomorrow. Peace."

Nahvi didn't give Meek a chance to respond to anything he said because he was tired of listening to his voice for one night. He needed to lie down and sleep on the shit that had happened. He'd get up the next day and regroup before he called Ashley to try and fix what had went down between them. He got in his ride and drove home, hoping to get himself some much needed sleep, but when he opened his door, all hell broke loose.

"Oh, so you finally want to show up after meeting with that cracker bitch."

"Monica, what the hell are you doing here? Better yet, how in the hell did you get in here? I remember taking your key, which means you don't have access in here anymore."

"Now you know I always get what I want. So, you should have nothing to question." She walked up to him seductively and stopped only when she couldn't go any further. At one time, her closeness would have caused Nahvi to rock the fuck up, but the thought of her touching him now had him disgusted to his inner core. She placed her hand on the print in his pants and when she realized he was still soft she backed away. If Nahvi would have still been the way he used to be, Monica would have been on her knees with the head of his dick touching the back of her throat, but he held no more feelings for her and she could sense it.

"Get out of my place, Monica, and don't ever bring your grimy ass back here again. If you see me in the streets or out with my girl, I suggest you turn and go in the opposite direction. I'm not playing these games with you, so I think you should move on. I do not want your ass. Now get the hell outta my space." He walked past her as if she were invisible and listened as the hateful slurs left her lips.

"You black ass motherfucker. I rode with your ass while you finished out that bid while others turned their back on you. Now you gonna kick me to the curb for another bitch like my feelings don't matter. I'll tell you this though. Every time I see your ass with that hoe ass cracker, I'm going to make you feel my presence. And I better not see you sell one piece of dope because if I do I'm going to—"

Nahvi was on her before she could finish her sentence. He went against everything he was taught and wrapped his hand around Monica's throat. He'd be damned if he let a bitch like her threaten his freedom. "You gonna what? Bitch, this is my last time telling you. Steer clear of me before those same people you wanna threaten me with finds your ass stickin' in a ditch." Nahvi's nose flared from anger while he took a breath and then he pushed Monica from his grasp and stated, "Get the hell outta my face and keep it that way."

The tears fell from her eyes while she looked at Nahvi defeated. She knew that she had fucked up for real and there was nothing she could do to fix it. She'd had high hopes for what they once shared and knew that it was all her fault for the way things ended between them. He had his back turned when he heard the door slam shut and let out a sigh of relief.

He knew that he had not seen the last of her. He just hoped that next time he did, he wouldn't have to put her six feet deep.

Chapter Eight

"Go ahead and say it, Tracey," Ashley blurted out as soon as they pulled into her apartment complex. She had waited the entire ride for Tracey to say that she had told her so, but her friend kept quiet.

"Damn, I hate that you know me so well, and since you do, I'm not gonna say it now. However, I will say that I'm sorry you had to go through what you did. It might have ended before it even started, but I'm telling you, Ash, that it is his loss, not yours. You are a strong woman and you'll overcome this the same way you have everything else in your life. The right man will come along. You just got to be patient."

Ashley smiled at her comment, but she wasn't feeling so strong. "I really felt a vibe with him, though. I don't know, Trace, it was just different than anything I've ever felt before, and it's strange because I felt it so quickly."

"Well, can I tell you what I want to feel? My man's arms wrapped around me in my warm bed. So, I'm gonna get outta here. I'll call and check on you in the morning, okay?"

"Okay, and thanks, Tracey." Ashley walked up the stairs to her door and when she opened it, the reality of her lonely life hit her. She started to wonder if she'd been too hard on Nahvi. She knew everybody had a past including her and she had no right to hold it against him. She told herself that when, or better yet, if he called again she would give him the benefit of the doubt. She placed her purse and keys down on the coffee table and sat down. She was so exhausted that she didn't even remove her shoes before she was fast asleep.

She opened her eyes to someone knocking loudly at her door. She couldn't believe that morning came so quickly and debated with herself on whether or not she wanted to answer the door. If it was Tracey, she wouldn't go away until she opened up. David worked in the daytime and Tracey would pop up as soon as he left. Ashley unhooked the latches and turned back around so she could find her way back to the couch to hopefully finish her slumber. She was surprised when the voice that spoke back to her didn't belong to her friend.

"Would you please give me a chance to explain about that shit that happened last night?"

"Nahvi? Oh my God. I thought you were Tracey. I just woke up and I haven't even brushed my teeth yet." She quickly covered her mouth with her hand and muffled her next words. "Uh, I'll be right back. Just let me go take care of this."

Nahvi laughed an infectious laugh while she ran to the bathroom. She looked in the mirror and noticed that she still had on her make up from the night before although a little smudged. After she brushed her teeth and washed her face, she felt a little more put together. She wasn't sure why she was making such an effort to fix herself, though. After all, she was supposed to be mad or disappointed or something, but she couldn't remember which one. Nahvi somehow already had that effect on her. When she was done getting herself together, she walked back in the living room but before she could get one word out of her mouth, Nahvi covered it with his.

Ashley tried with all her strength to pull back from him, but a force greater than the one she possessed held her there. She savored the taste of his tongue as it lashed out against hers. The softness of his lips were like the clouds she had imagined in heaven to be. Even when he broke the kiss and pulled back from her, she could still feel him. She opened her eyes and looked into his and tried to say something, but no words came out, so he spoke instead.

"I'm sorry, Ash, but I couldn't help myself. Your ass shouldn't be so damn pretty."

Ashley finally found the strength to speak. "Nahvi, you do know that was uncalled for, right? However, I can't even be mad at you because that was wonderful. I almost forgot how it feels to be kissed."

"There's plenty more where that came from."

"No. No. No. Nahvi, we need to talk about last night. You know, about the drama with your so-called ex. If that's really what she is."

Nahvi scrunched his eyebrows and rubbed his chin before he responded to the comment, "Look, I don't know what type of nigga you think I am, but I don't play two women at the same time. Maybe that's the type of men you're used to but don't judge me by what the last man done to you. That shit ain't fair, ma."

She knew that he was right because she didn't want him to hold anything like that against her either. "You know what? You're right. I can't judge you by what others have done, but it just seems as if all the men I've had in my life turned out to be dogs, and although you haven't told me what you do for a living, I somehow feel like I already know. Them thugs left me with a sour taste in my mouth because of all the bullshit and drama that follows them. So, what makes you any different?"

Nahvi did it again … licked those lips like he was about to eat a juicy melon and looked at Ashley like she was that melon. She could feel her panties moisten and knew that there was nothing she could do to stop it. When he spoke, she could feel his voice deep down in her soul. "Well, I'm different because I can sweeten that sour taste they left behind. Let me show you how a real thug treats his lady."

She heard what he'd said but was still skeptical. She had been made so many promises only for them to be broken before they were even sealed. Nahvi seemed so sincere with his words and as he waited for her response, she could see the anticipation in his eyes. She needed someone who could love her with all they had inside and somehow, she felt that he would. Ashley knew that there was no way she could turn him down.

"Nahvi, I'm going to forget about what happened last night because I know it was a surprise for you also. I'm going to give you another chance because I feel like you deserve one. However, because of what you are into, and you don't have to admit it because I really don't wanna know. You can make up last night by promising me that you'll keep your street business exactly where it's at, in the streets."

"Come on, ma, you know you too precious to put in harm's way. Besides, I'm ready to pull up out of that street shit and go legit. I got a few more loose ends to tie up and then I'm out for good. In a few months, you'll never have to worry about that street shit again."

Ashley had heard so many dope boys claim they were going to give up the life, but that shit ran through their veins. That fast money was hard to let go of once you started making it, and deep down, she felt like Nahvi would be no different. However, no matter what she said, Ashley knew that she would ride with him and stand by whatever decision he made, even if it was the wrong one.

Chapter Nine

"Yo, Nahvi, what that snow bunny think about you being out here in these streets delivering packages and selling poison to the people? You sure she's ready to be a dealer's wife?"

Nahvi looked at Meek like he'd lost his damn mind and then answered his question. "Damn, Meek, a nigga ain't even had the pussy yet and you trying to marry me off. The fuck's up with that?"

"Nigga, you ain't dived in the cookie jar yet and your ass already getting soft out here. Shit, she's all you talk about now. Nigga, you done lost your touch. You might as well go door to door and put a brick in front of each one. You let Bruno get away with being short on that gwop. You was supposed to bust that ass like you used to do but you talkin' bout 'Nah B, you good. We'll make it up on the next one.'"

Nahvi couldn't say shit because Meek was right. Something inside of him had changed just in the short amount of time that Ashley had been in his life. He used to bust a nigga's cap for being short on his money but lately, that money had become less important. However, he decided that it would be the last time he'd let someone slip on his flow. He had lost sight of what he was doing and told himself that he would get back on track. "Aye, I only did that because Bruno's always been good business even before I caught that case that sent me away. A nigga ain't went soft, just showing some appreciation, that's all."

"Appreciation? Nigga, you ain't supposed to show no appreciation in these fucking streets. You been doing this shit a long time and you know how these muthafuckas get down. They take that shit for a weakness, and once becomes twice and then there's a third time. You been doing this shit almost all your life, so you know it better than me, dawg. You one of the greatest that's ever did it. You can't be letting shit like that go. That white girl got your head all fucked up, my man. You need to take a minute and regroup and then try this shit again."

Nahvi and Ashley had been getting along so good and had been drama-free ever since that incident with Monica. Nahvi wasn't trying to mess that up but he did need to get his mind right. He still had intentions of leaving the game for good, but his goal was still a few months off. He decided that he would start putting in more time in the streets but first, he had to figure out a good way to tell Ashley he wouldn't be around as much, and he only hoped that she understood.

"You right, Meek, I have been a little off my game lately, but I'm 'bout to wake the fuck up and get back right."

"Yeah, and what you gonna tell ya' girl? She's gonna be okay with that? Because from what you already told me, she ain't too keen on being with another street nigga. What if she ain't down with the plan?"

"What you mean? She already knew what it was when we first started out. She gon' be cool so chill out with that questioning."

Meek could sense Nahvi's frustration so he tried to explain his logic. "Nahvi, look. When you out here physically you gotta to be out here mentally too. That's all I'm saying. You know that shit can go from sweet to sour at the snap of a finger when your mind is wandering in other places. Now I'm not saying to forget about your girl or nothing like that but when you out in these trenches, they got to be your priority. Your mind can't be in two places at once so you need to establish between the two. You a smart nigga and so far, you been successful at this shit. I don't want your ass to get caught slippin' because your mind is on the other side of town. I got your back one hundred percent, but I need to know that you got mine too."

"I always got your back, Meek. You the nigga that gave me a second chance and even gave me my spot back although you ain't even know me. I'll eat a bullet for you and even feed one to another muthafucka for you. You my dawg, man, and don't worry 'bout me, I'ma get back on track. You ain't even got to tell me twice."

Meek raised his eyebrows and gave Nahvi some dap. "Yeah, and I'ma hold you to what you saying. Now let's get the hell outta here."

Meek dropped Nahvi off at his condo although his ride was parked at Ashley's. He had money and product on him and had given her his word that he'd never show up to her place dirty or with evidence from the streets. He'd call her the next morning to come pick him up because it was really late, and he didn't want to disturb her. He just hoped that he didn't regret his decision.

Corey Robinson

Chapter Ten

Monica had been staying with Tonya until she could get back on her feet and although that was her friend, she couldn't wait to move the hell out. Tonya had a fifteen-month-old son and used Monica like a live-in babysitter, making her realize why she'd never had children of her own. It had been a little over a month since her and Nahvi had broken up and she was miserable without him. She had been messing around with random niggas but none of them seemed to stack up to him. She knew that she had really fucked up but still hoped that one day, he'd realize he couldn't live without her and give her another chance.

She was sitting on Tonya's sofa when she heard the key in the lock. Tonya had been out shopping at the expense of her baby daddy and had left Monica with her brat. A bitch like Monica didn't have time nor patience to be changing shitty diapers and was too damn classy to let one of them little bastards puke on her clothes. She didn't understand why Tonya didn't take him with them but when she explained it, Monica finally caught on. "Girl, I am trying to get me some dick too and his little ass ain't gonna do nothing but cock block. I won't be gone long." Tonya had given her the same excuse every time. Monica wondered why she never invited him inside. Surely he would want to spend time with his son but she chalked it up to Tonya not wanting him around her. She knew that Tonya's baby daddy was a trick ass nigga and he would probably try to fuck her too, but Tonya didn't have to worry because Monica didn't want that dirty dick inside of her.

As soon as Tonya walked in, Monica became a little envious. Her hands were full of bags with designer labels on them and made her think of the days when Nahvi spoiled her.

"Bitch, you don't got to show boat with all those bags. Been there, done that."

Tonya looked at her like she was crazy and then sat the bags on the coffee table in front of her as if she were trying to rub it in even more. "Well, then I guess you don't want this little bit of information that I found out about Nahvi's little snow princess."

"What? Bitch, you better tell me everything."

At first, Tonya acted like she had nothing to say but she was a nosy bitch and loved to gossip so Monica knew she wouldn't be able to hold it in for much longer. "Well, it turns out that Kelvin's ex and Nahvi's new bitch are one in the same. All those times he called himself dissin' me, he was running to that hoe."

"Hell no. He told you all this?"

"Now do you really think his ass is going to tell on himself? Kelvin's ass thinks he's too smart and a bitch can't find out other ways. His homeboy Trent that's been trying to get in my jeans all these years spilled the beans for a little taste of this honey. So, before Kelvin dropped me off I put a little bug in his ear."

"So how in the hell does that mean anything to me? How is that going to get me my man back, and bitch, when did you let Trent taste the goodies?"

Monica knew that there was always a method to Tonya's madness and she made sure she revealed it. "Well, I made him a promise for the weekend, and with that long ass tongue he has in his mouth, I'm going to keep that promise."

"Ugh, I don't care about that, just tell me how that information helps me."

"Okay, girl, damn. Well, Kelvin and Nahvi used to be rivals before Nahvi went to prison. Something to do with some territory issue, but as far as I know, that beef was never squashed. For Kelvin to find out that his enemy is fucking with someone he used to smash, it's going to get real ugly."

"Uh, bitch, I don't want Nahvi in some damn street beef, and why would Kelvin care about that if he ain't fucking with the girl anymore?"

"Now come on, Moni, you know how these niggas can be about a bitch whether they still fuck with them or not. Nahvi messing with that girl after she's done been with Kelvin is against the rules."

"So, you are basically sending your child's father back to the bitch he was fucking while he was fucking with you too. That shit don't even sound right."

"Fuck Kelvin's ass, girl, I never wanted him. That shit that happened between us was just supposed to be a quick nut but my ass ended up pregnant, so now I got to put up with his ass for eighteen fucking years. Bitch, if his money wasn't as long as it is, I would be telling him to kiss my ass, but I'm going to milk him for everything I can and send him back to Monique dry."

The two women shared a laugh at the expense of what Toya had said. Monique was Kelvin's other baby momma and they had an eighteen month old daughter together. Kelvin had been fucking both of them at the same time and the news that he'd did it while he was with that white bitch made Monica feel like she could win the battle after all.

She jumped up from the couch and grabbed her purse and gave Tonya puppy dog eyes. "Can I please borrow your car? There's something I need to do."

Tonya was hesitant at first but finally gave in and pulled them from her purse. Monica was about to go on a mission and she hoped that she could accomplish what she set out to do. She couldn't sit back any longer and allow the bitch to have what rightfully belonged to her, Nahvi was hers and it was time she made him realize that he couldn't live without her.

Chapter Eleven

Ashley was so worried about Nahvi that she found it hard to go to sleep. He had never stayed out so late and she couldn't help but think about all the bad things that could happen to him out in the streets. She had hoped that he would have come in early because she had a special night planned for him. She would start off with his favorite meal of home fried chicken, baked macaroni and cheese and some collard greens seasoned with fat back. The freshly baked apple pie would make the meal complete. She had spent all evening preparing it and it had gotten cold waiting for him to return. Once she got him good and full she would ask him to join her in the bathtub where she would go underwater and explore all his inches and then she'd let him make love to her for the first time. Nahvi knew that he'd already taken her by storm and although she said that she would save herself until a man put a ring on it, she somehow felt like he would be the one she'd marry.

Ashley thought that she would never love again after the way that Kelvin had done her but JaNahvi Karter had opened up something inside of her that she never knew existed. The short time they had shared together made her realize that she never wanted to let him go. He had convinced her that he would soon retire from the streets and she believed him but lately, he had been in them even more. She knew in her heart that she would stick by him, even if he stuck by the streets.

She was about to close her eyes when she heard a light knock at her door. She had meant to give him a key to her place so that he could come and go as he pleased. She wanted him to always feel like he was welcomed. She pulled off the sweatpants that she'd had on and then her bra, leaving her with a t-shirt and panties. She was upset with him coming in so late but not so upset that she would hold out on her desires.

On her way to the door, she lit the scented candles that she'd placed around the apartment to set the tone. She couldn't wait to feel his manhood inside of her so that they could become one. Ashley unlocked the door and opened it with a seductive look in her eyes and a wetness between her legs, but as soon as she saw who was on the other side she wanted to run and hide.

"Kelvin? What in the hell are you doing here? I thought I told you to never come by here again."

He looked her up and down and then licked his lips like he used to do right before he devoured her. "The fuck is up with you and JaNahvi Karter?"

"Uh. I don't owe you an explanation for anything or anyone I'm doing. Now if you'll excuse me." She tried to shut the door but Kelvin put his foot in the way and stopped it from closing. He pushed it back open and almost stumbled, but he quickly wrapped his arms around Ashley to break his fall.

She had been in love with Kelvin at one time or at least she thought she had been, and his closeness almost took her breath away. She stared into his eyes, speechless as her heart beat ninety miles an hour. The man that held her in his arms had hurt her over and over again, but she just couldn't find the energy to hate him.

"Come on, Ash, you know a nigga's still feeling you. We could have worked that shit out."

She finally found the strength to push him away. She had been jilted by him so many times and needed to stand up and let him know that shit would never be sweet between them again. "Kelvin, I walked in on you with another bitch laid up in the same bed that we shared. You held no regards for how I felt, so how the hell could we have possibly worked that out?"

"Ash, you know I love your white ass, but I get weak sometimes."

"Weak? You don't get weak, Kelvin. You're just a piece of shit that likes slinging your dick everywhere. You had two babies on me by two different women after you told me that we should wait to start a family. I forgave you for a lot of shit, but when I walked in that day and caught your dirty ass dick in another woman, there was no taking your ass back. You're just a disrespectful motherfucker."

"Yeah, but how the hell you gonna move on with my fucking enemy? Where the hell is your loyalty at?"

Ashley thought that Kelvin had lost his mind if he believed she owed him some loyalty. "You have room to talk about loyalty when you were the one who cheated on me! Besides, it ain't like I knew that Nahvi was your enemy, and even if I would have, anything I do shouldn't concern you anymore. You know that I always stayed out of your street businesses. Being with him wasn't intentional."

Kelvin started to say something else, but Tracey walked in and crippled him of his words. "Oh hell no. What is he doing here?"

Kelvin asked, "I could be asking the same thing about you. Ain't you got a man to be home with while you over here all in our business?"

"Business? You ain't got no damn business with her. She has done moved on and forgot about your ass so I suggest you go on and find you some more bitches to have babies with." Tracey walked back to the door and opened it, making Kelvin feel like head been defeated.

Ashley wasn't sure why she had shown up but at that moment she was so glad that she did. Kelvin looked back and forth from Ashley to Tracey, and when he saw that it was a no-win situation he walked out, but not before he got another word in. "You'll see me again. In the meantime, you can tell that nigga I'm coming for mine."

Tracey slammed the door shut behind him and made sure to lock it, and then she drilled Ashley. "Girl, what in the hell was Kelvin doing here this time of night, and you better not tell me you're thinking of taking him back."

"Really, Tracey? I'm not that dumb girl anymore. His ass just showed up calling himself checking me about Nahvi. Apparently, they have some sort of beef going on between them."

"Hmmm, and Nahvi hasn't mentioned that to you? I wonder why."

"Uh, maybe because I haven't talked to him about Kelvin. I mean, he knows about all the bullshit I went through with my ex, but I never told him his name. I just never thought it was important. And what the hell are you doing here anyway? Don't be trying to put all the focus on me and my drama. Is something going on with you and David?"

Tracey sat down on the couch with a disappointed look on her face and told Ashley everything. "Girl, I'm just not feeling his ass anymore. I mean, we have been together since high school and it's been really good for the most part, but my ass is beginning to get bored. We always have the same routine and there's no excitement. Ash, the dick don't even feel good to me anymore. I don't know, it's just not as good as it used to be."

"Wow, I'm sorry, Trace. I know you really love David and y'all have been together a long ass time, but you're supposed to be happy, and if you're not happy anymore then I support whatever you do." Ashley reached over and gave her friend a hug. Tracey had always been there for her through all of the heartbreaks, so she knew that she needed to return the same sentiments.

When their embrace broke, Tracey completely shocked Ashley with what came out of her mouth next, because it was damn squire unexpected. "Hey, you think you could get Nahvi to hook me up with his boy Meek?"

"What? Are you serious? Since when did you start liking black dick?"

"Girl, please. I been curious for a minute now. I'm trying to find out what all the fuss is about. Besides, since David's sex game is so predictable and doesn't satisfy me anymore, I might as well move on to bigger things. I need some excitement in my life, and I am not going to get it staying with his ass. I think some of that thug mentality would set me straight. So, can you hook a girl up?"

"Yeah, I'll see what I can do. He did ask about you once but I told him you had a man, so he never asked again. He said that he wasn't trying to break up any happy homes."

"Bitch, you never told me that. I should be mad at your ass, but since you gonna work on it I'm gonna let that slide. Where is Nahvi, anyway? Does he always stay out like that?"

Tracey's question caught Ashley off guard and reminded her that she still hadn't heard from him. "No, he's usually in from the block by now, at least when he stays over here. I'm a little worried about him. Maybe I should call." Ashley picked up her phone and dialed Nahvi's number but it went straight to voicemail. "Dammit. His phone sent me to voicemail. That's not like him not to answer. Maybe his phone died or something. Let me call Meek." Ashley could see Tracey's face light up at the mention of his name and shook her head. She was acting like a schoolgirl with her first crush.

Meek answered on the second ring, "Sup, Ash, everything cool?"

"Yeah, Meek, at least I hope so. I just called Nahvi's phone and it went to voicemail. Is he with you? It's not like him to not answer my call."

"Nah, ya' nigga ain't with me. I just dropped him off at his place. He said he didn't want to disturb you this late, plus, he wanted to get cleaned up. His ass probably done fell asleep or something. I'm sure he'll call you as soon as he gets up. Stop worrying so much. Nahvi ain't going nowhere."

"Yeah, I guess you're right. It's just not like him. I'll drive his truck over there in the morning. Thanks, Meek." Ashley started to hang up, but Tracey looked at her funny as if to say what's up. "Oh, Meek, I forgot to mention something. My friend Tracey said what's up with you and her chillin' sometime?"

"She said that?" Meek asked in his debonair manner.

"Yep, that's what she said."

"You tell her that we can chill whenever she wants, but I ain't that lame ass white boy she been laying beside. I'ma put some real dick in her life."

"Oh, yeah, I'm sure she can't wait for that. I'll let her know. Talk to you later, Meek." Ashley turned to her friend and smiled and told her exactly what she wanted to hear. "Bitch, Meek is ready to lay it down. He said y'all can chill whenever you ready."

"Yes. Oh my God. Am I gonna be able to handle all that dick they say black men are packing? You know I've only ever been with David."

"I don't know if you can handle it or not, but you better be ready because once you go black, bitch you'll never go back." The two shared a laugh about the old saying that had proven to be true so many times. A sadness suddenly came over Ashley. "Hey, Trace, you more than welcome to crash but Meek said he took Nahvi home. He didn't want to disturb me so late, plus, he still had that shit on him but I don't want to wait 'til morning to see him so I'm gonna fix my man a plate and go over there. I'll try to be back before lunch, so just make yourself at home."

Ashley went in her kitchen and fixed Nahvi a plate of food. She was sure he'd be starving after a long night on the block. She planned to feed him, fuck him and rock him to sleep. She grabbed the keys to the Denali which also had his spare door key on it. She was going to surprise her man, but little did she know, she would be the one surprised.

Corey Robinson

Chapter Twelve

Nahvi knew that he should have called Ashley because he knew her so well. She would have been worried by now, but he was just so tired and wanted to get some sleep. It had been a long night on the block and also a slow one. Slower than it had been in a while. Nahvi went to lay down on his couch but his stomach growled and reminded him that he hadn't eaten since earlier. He walked to his kitchen and opened the refrigerator although he already knew what he would find. When he saw the six pack of Corona and the empty butter dish he made a note to himself that he needed to go shopping. He'd get Ashley to go with him to help him out on what to stock. He'd never had to keep much food on hand because Monica damn sure didn't cook. It had been so long since he'd had a home cooked meal and just the thought of one had his stomach crying out again.

Nahvi had been spending so much time at Ashley's place that he'd neglected his own. He decided that he would put it all out there and ask her to move in with him although he wasn't sure she'd want to live in the same place he'd shared with Monica. If not, she could call up a realtor and find them a nice home. He didn't care, as long as they were together.

Since Nahvi's stomach had to wait, he turned his focus on the king sized bed in his massive bedroom. He had gotten used to sleeping in it alone but told himself that he would invest in a new one because when Ashley finally decided to give him the goodies, he didn't want to give it to her in the same bed he had given it to Monica in. He got completely naked and while he turned the air conditioning down to sixty, he put his mattress temperature up to seventy-five. No sooner than he laid his head on the plush pillow, he was out.

The warm, wet sensation on his dick made him feel like he was stuck in a wet dream. He wanted to open his eyes, but he was too afraid the feeling would go away if he did. He reached down to his dick and when he felt someone's hair, he quickly opened his eyes. "The fuck." When Nahvi saw Monica's head bouncing on his manhood he pushed her and quickly jumped out of the bed. "Bitch, what in the hell are you doing?"

Monica ignored his question and lay back on the bed the way she used to do right before she put on a show. Her naked form glistened under the dim light, and when she spread her legs and touched herself, Nahvi could see the wetness at her opening. His dick stood at attention as she guided one of her fingers inside herself. He could have sworn that his balls were going to burst but there was no way he would let Monica do what she wanted. He was saving all those seeds for Ashley.

He grabbed a pair of sweatpants and put them on and then grabbed Monica's arm, pulling her up from the bed. "You know you foul, right? Get your clothes on and get the hell outta here."

"Ah, come on, Nahvi, you know my mouth felt good on that dick, and you know this pussy is going to feel even better." Monica reached out to touch him but he slapped it away. She was no longer his weakness and she needed to realize that.

"You can't be doing shit like this, Monica. You know I got someone else in my life now. I didn't cheat on you when we were together and I'm damn sure not going to cheat on her either. Now get out and leave me the hell alone."

Monica grabbed her clothes with an attitude and while she put them on, she also put Nahvi onto something he didn't know. "Yeah, I know you got someone else, but did she tell you that her ex is Kelvin Brown? Oops, she must have left that little bit of information out, boo."

"Hold up. What the fuck is you talking about? Where you get some bullshit like that from?"

"Well, you do know that Kelvin has a son by Tonya and come to find out, she had that son with him while he was still with your precious little snowflake. Yeah, that nigga actually had two babies on that hoe. Don't you think she should have shared that information with you?"

As bad as Nahvi didn't want to believe her he could tell by the look in her eyes that she was telling the truth. He was pissed at the revelation because him and Kelvin had a beef that started before Nahvi got locked up and it had never been squashed.

The beef started when Nahvi and one of his boys were on a run. When they got to the drop off spot, Kelvin was there with his crew. "Yo, playa, you can turn around and go back the way you came. This my spot now. Your services are no longer needed."

Nahvi's boy was about to pull out his burner but Nahvi stopped him because the spot Kelvin wanted didn't bring in enough money to cause bloodshed. However, that wasn't the only spot Kelvin wanted. He had planned to take over the entire territory. Nahvi had run into one of Kelvin's boys and put a whooping on his ass. He was ready for war if they wanted to bring it but instead of a war, the police showed up and arrested him for assault and the judge sentenced him to eight years.

Nahvi hadn't had a problem with Kelvin since he'd been released but once he found out he was seeing Ashley, it would start their beef right back up. Nahvi was upset that he had to hear that bit of news from Monica's grimy ass instead of Ashley. Moncia had known what went down with him and

Kelvin and now Nahvi wondered if Ashley really did too. His paranoia set in and he began to wonder if Ashley was only with him as a get back for all Kelvin had done to her.

Nahvi looked at Monica and felt sick on his stomach but didn't want her to pick up on how the news made him feel. "Monica, just leave. I really need you to get the hell outta my sight. I know you trying to start some shit between me and my girl but just so you know, even if I ain't with her, I still don't want your trifling ass."

Nahvi walked to his front door and pulled it open with the force of a beast. He needed Monica out of his face. He was already angry and her presence was only making it worse. No sooner than he swung the door open, Ashley appeared with an aluminum foil covered plate in her hand and walked right into Monica. She looked back and forth from Nahvi to his ex and when she noticed he didn't have a shirt on her eyes trailed down his torso until she got to the print in his sweatpants. His dick was no longer hard but because of the size and the way it lay against his thigh, Ashley didn't know any better.

Monica smiled at Ashley and then turned to Nahvi. "Aw, look, she brought you something to eat. Too bad you're already full," and then she walked out leaving them alone.

Nahvi could see the tears form in Ashley's eyes but his anger outweighed any sympathy he could find. "Why didn't you tell me that your ex was Kelvin Brown?"

"What? What the hell does Kelvin have to do with anything? And while you're worried about him, why didn't you call and tell me that you were over here frolicking with her and that was why you didn't come home to me? What's the matter, Nahvi? You couldn't hold out any longer on some pussy so you called in a substitute? Or better yet, am I the substitute?"

He let out a long sigh and turned his back to her so he could sit down and get his mind right. He closed his eyes when he felt her come close to him but opened them back up when he heard her sit the plate down.

"I was going to give myself to you tonight, but you never showed up. I even made you your favorite dish, but you know what Nahvi? I can't do this with you so tell that bitch she can have you!"

Nahvi didn't seem to care that Ashley had walked out on him because he felt like she was in the wrong for not letting him know about Kelvin. She had made her own bed so now, she could lie in it.

After his fall out with Ashley, Nahvi dove deeper into the streets. He rarely stayed at home and didn't give a fuck about anything.

"Aye, Nahvi, man. Why you think Monica told you that bullshit?"

"Nigga, do I look like I give a fuck about why she told me that? Ashley was dead ass wrong for not giving me that information and you know I can't let that shit go. I feel like anything we shared was staged just to get some pay back to that muthafucka. I feel like her ass used me and I can't let that shit go."

"Did you ever mention to Ashley that you had a beef going on with Kelvin's ass?"

"Nah, man, the subject just never came up but that ain't no excuse. She still should have put me up on game."

Nahvi thought back to the night that Ashley walked up on Monica as she was leaving his place. He expected her to show her ass, but she was so calm that it actually scared him. He had been so used to being cursed out by the sistas he'd done wrong but Ashley handled that shit like a real lady. He began to wonder if he was too hard on her, but those thoughts went out the window as soon as Meek pulled into the 7-Eleven. Nahvi noticed Kelvin's pearl white Mercedes truck and got out. By the time he got close to the ride, Kelvin walked out of the store.

"You looking for me, playa? I know you ain't out here to check me about no bitch."

Nahvi didn't even respond but instead walked up on him and punched him in the mouth.

Meek came out of the store after seeing what he had done and ran over to where Nahvi was at, rubbing on his fist. "Nahvi, nigga, have you lost your damn mind? Get in the truck, man. We gotta get the hell outta here."

His nose flared as he looked down at Kelvin who was wiping the blood from his lip. Nahvi knew that what he'd just done was going to bring up some old shit but at that moment, he didn't give a fuck what it caused. If Kelvin wanted to bring it, he could because Nahvi and his crew would damn sure be ready.

"Man, what the hell is wrong with you? Don't you know that nigga is going to come for us now? The hell was you thinking?"

"So, let that bitch come. I got something real hot for his ass when he does."

"Yo, you need to get your shit together because I ain't ready to die, and at the rate you going, you gonna get our asses killed. You better call that girl or something because shit like this ain't gon' work for me."

Nahvi was a thug with a broken heart and because he'd never had one before, he had no idea how to handle it. When Meek pulled into the parking lot, Nahvi jumped out without saying one word to him. He knew that his boy was pissed and honestly, he couldn't blame him. He had fucked up, and as bad as he didn't want to admit it, he was dead ass wrong. He swore that he could still smell Ashley's scent and that made him even angrier. He started to feel like maybe he should have listened to her because there was a chance that she wasn't really using him as payback. Maybe she was really feeling him. Nahvi didn't want to dwell on what had happened so he decided to do what any other man would have done when shit went sideways. He was going to get some pussy. Ashley may not have wanted to give it up, but he knew plenty of bitches who would.

Corey Robinson

Chapter Thirteen

"Oh, Ash. I am so sorry this shit happened like that. I know you had high hopes for you and him, but girl you should never put all your eggs in one basket. You should always keep you some options open."

Ashley rolled her eyes at Tracey's comment because it all sounded like a bunch of shit. She had room to talk because the only option she'd ever had was David. It was Ashley who had her heartbroken over and over. "Fuck that, I'm done with men. I just can't keep going through this kind of crap. I don't know, Trace, maybe it was meant for me to be alone."

"No, don't say that. Ya' know I talk a lot of shit about you and them damn thugs but I know that's what you like. You've just been picking the wrong ones. However, I honestly think that Nahvi could have been the one."

"Bitch, you're only saying that now because you want to hook up with Meek. You wasn't agreeing with it a few weeks ago, and besides, how could I possibly ever look at Nahvi the same? All I can think about is that bitch coming out of his condo while he stood there half naked."

Tracey raised her eyebrows because she felt that Ashley may have over exaggerated the situation. "How do you know that something happened between them? Did it look like they had been getting busy?"

Ashley thought about the question and the image of Nahvi's dick print in those sweatpants kept popping up in her vision. "I don't know. I mean, Monica actually looked like she was pissed off about something and whatever it was, happened before I got there."

"Ash, why don't you call him and see if y'all can talk, because I'm tired of watching you mope around here. Go over there and give that man some pussy and let him know who's boss."

"Bitch, pussy don't fix nothin'."

"Shit, it kept David in his place all these years so you can tell that to somebody who don't know any better."

"Whatever, but I am not going over there and throwing pussy in his face. Bitch, that would be like a reward or something, not punishment."

"Punishment. Come on, Ash, Nahvi is what, thirty-five years old, not eight. You crazy as hell if you don't go get your man because as soon as Meek shows up for me, I'm outta here."

No sooner than Tracey got the words out of her mouth someone knocked on the door. Ashley hoped that it was Nahvi but knew that she would be disappointed when she opened it. "Oh, hey Meek. You by yourself?"

Meek smiled and walked in before he answered Ashley's question. "Yeah, I had to drop Nahvi's lovesick ass at home. That nigga done lost his damn mind. Yo, Ash, you need to go over there so y'all can work that shit out. My nigga ain't the same."

"How do you expect us to work anything out when he won't even listen to me? And besides, he's the one who had another bitch in his house. I'm not going through that shit with nobody else. That bitch can have him!"

"Yeah, that would be all cool if he wanted her too, but he ain't studying her ass. She snuck in and caught his ass off guard but ain't nothing happened between them. Come on, give my boy some credit."

Ashley stood and thought about what Meek had just told her and wondered if he was telling the truth or just covering for his friend. Maybe she had jumped to conclusions about why Monica was there. All she knew was that she had grown tired of being done any kind of way. She couldn't help the fact that she was drawn to bad boys and had been all her life. She loved the ruggedness and hard outer shell because she knew that deep inside them was a real lover boy just waiting to come out. Ashley needed that toughness they carried because it made her feel protected when she was at her weakest and couldn't protect herself.

She couldn't lie to herself. She missed the hell out of Nahvi but she didn't want to seem naive or make him feel that he could do her any kind of way and get away with it. She had continuously tried to call him only to be sent to voicemail and she wondered what that meant. Did he even miss her or feel remotely bad about what happened? She knew in her heart that there was only one way to find out and she was determined to get the answer.

Corey Robinson

Chapter Fourteen

Nahvi sat in the VIP booth and watched all the dancers as they slung their titties and bounced their asses. He took a sip of his drink and rubbed on his dick as the thick redbone made her way over to him. He didn't break his stare when she stopped in front of him and put one of her high heeled feet up on his knee. He smiled a devious smile and the bitch in front of him smiled back. He knew it was because of his hood status. It was no secret that JaNahvi Karter was the nigga to see but if the half naked woman that grinded her hips only inches from his face thought she was gonna hook him, she had another thing coming.

He began to imagine that it was Ashley in front of him instead of a complete stranger. He couldn't lie to himself any longer, he damn sure missed her white ass, but he just wasn't certain that he could look over the fact that one of his rivals had her first. How would he be able to look past that and not feel some type of way?

The dancer in front of him pulled her thong to the side revealing a cleanly shaved pussy. Her lips were fat and Nahvi admired the small circle that pierced her swollen clit. She used both of her hands to spread the folds so he could watch as her finger disappeared into her wetness. When she pulled it out, she reached over to run it under his nose, but before she could get close to the flesh above his top lip, he grabbed her wrist and startled her.

"What's the matter? Don't you like the smell of wet pussy?"

He laughed at her question but never answered. He instead stood up and towered over her small frame. With his hand still around her small wrist helped her to one of the VIP rooms where he hoped to get more than just a smell of her essence.

The room was furnished with a nice sized bed and had a small bathroom to the side. The mini bar was stocked with enough alcohol to get an entire army drunk. He had paid for the room in advance but wanted to make sure he picked out the right girl to share it with. The redbone had caught his attention as soon as he walked in, however, he would sit there and wait until she found him to make a move.

His dick was rocked the fuck up and he couldn't wait to release the beast from his boxer briefs. He locked the door and turned on the music before he spoke. "Take that shit off and show a nigga what you really working with."

The dancer was hesitant at first because she was used to getting her money up front, but she thought about who she was dealing with and knew that if she acted right, her g-string would be laced the fuck up by the end of the night. She would be the envy of all the other dancers because she was the one JaNahvi Karter chose. She vowed to put on a performance that no one else could ever do because she wanted to make sure he never requested anyone else but her.

As the music flowed from the speakers, she wound her hips and looked Nahvi in the eyes. When she reached up and untied the straps of her top it fell from around her neck and revealed the nicest set of implants that Nahvi had ever seen. Her half dollar sized areolas were a shade darker than her skin, and if her nipples would have been bullets, he would be a dead man. He lifted a lone finger and gave her the come here signal. On her slow, sensual walk across the small room, she untied the remaining straps and let the top fall to the floor.

Nahvi felt like being a dog ass nigga so when she got in front of him, he guided her movements. "Them mufuckas is long and fat. Come on and pull one into your mouth. Let me see how you work that tongue."

She knew that she would have been a fool to deny him his pleasure, so she lifted one of her breasts to her mouth and stuck out her tongue. She never broke eye contact when she pulled a nipple between her lips and noticed that Nahvi didn't blink one time. She just knew that she had him right where she wanted him. When she released her hardened nipple, she turned her back to him and looped her fingers around the small strings that held her g-string together. She pushed down and bent over slowly at the same time. Her ass cheeks opened enough for Nahvi to see the small hole that peeked at him. When she reached her hands behind her and opened her fat injected mounds, she could feel a brush of wind move across her wetness.

"A nigga wanna see something hard slide up in that pussy so go on over there and lie on that bed for me."

She once again did as she was told and when she lied back, she made sure to spread her legs as wide as they would go. She couldn't wait to brag to the other women about how good JaNahvi Karter's dick felt inside of her. Just the thought made her wanna cum right then. "Come on and fuck me baby. This pussy is so wet just thinking about you inside of it."

Nahvi stood from the chair that he had sat in and instead of walking to the bed where she lay at, he walked to the door and unlocked it. He noticed the confused look on her face and answered her question without her even asking it. "Don't worry, lil momma. You gon' get some dick, it just won't be this one."

The dancer's eyes grew big as two other men walked in the room. When they saw her on the bed, they both smiled and began to get undressed. "She's all your boys. Make sure you fuck her real good." Nahvi stated and walked out. The old him would have fucked her in every orifice of her body but something inside of him had changed. He didn't even want to stay and watch, which was what he had originally planned to do. His mind just wasn't feeling it and although he wanted to bust a nut in something warm, he couldn't bring himself to do it.

He walked out of the club and the cool night breeze told him that the seasons were about to change. Fall was his favorite time of year because he could rock his flyest gear and not have to worry about being uncomfortable in the Georgia heat. He decided to hit the block and see what was going on. It was Friday night so he knew the fiends would be out in droves looking for their next hit. There was plenty of money to be made and what better way to spend his time than lacing his jeans?

When he pulled up on the block, all the crackheads ran toward his truck, although he had told them time and time again not to bring that kind of attention. Usually, he would have gotten out and cursed them the fuck out but he welcomed it. He felt like he had no one else so he embraced his hood fame like a real star. Nahvi was feeling real generous so had his boy, Troll bless the fiends with what they were looking for.

"Damn my nigga, you just want me to give it away like that? The fuck is wrong with you?"

"Nah bitch, what the fuck is wrong with you? That's my shit you out here pushing to pay your bills so don't question what the fuck I do with it. If you got a problem, I can help someone else pay they bills instead."

Troll held his hands up in surrender and then did as Nahvi told him to do. He couldn't wait to see Meek and tell him what went down. He knew that he was going to be pissed and would check Nahvi for the foolishness. Troll had been working for Meek since he first came to Atlanta and set up shop, but when Nahvi was released from prison and Meek passed him back the reins, a lot of the rules changed. Troll had no choice but to respect what Nahvi had told him to do if he wanted to keep his spot on the block.

Nahvi walked up to the porch of the trap house that some of him and Meeks crew worked out of. He knew that he had caught them by surprise, so he wasn't shocked at what he found when he walked inside.

"Monica. The fuck you doing up in my shit?"

Monica sucked her teeth and smiled at him as if he already knew the answer, but he was stoked because he'd never allowed her here when they were together. When she rolled her eyes, he pushed her against the wall and his hand quickly found her throat. "Bitch, when I ask you a question, you fucking answer it. Now, what the hell are you doing up in my shit?"

Suddenly, a voice came from behind him. "Aye yo, playa, she with me."

Nahvi released Monica from his grip and turned around. When he saw Jared, he scrunched his brows and asked him the same thing. "Well, then I guess I should be asking your wife what the hell you doing up in my shit with this bitch."

"Yo man, I ain't come here looking for no trouble. I just came to pick up a little something, but we can make it whatever you want it to be as long as you keep my wife outta this."

Nahvi looked from Jared to Monica and decided that the bitch wasn't worth it. Plus, he didn't want to bring any heat to his boys. He looked around the room and saw that all his men had their hand on a burner just in case he gave them the order to clap Jared's ass but Nahvi brushed that shit off his shoulder and said. "Go on and get the hell outta here and next time you need something from here, leave that bitch outside."

When Nahvi first encountered Jared and Monica at the club together, he remembered how Jared pulled out his piece and pointed it at him but now that he was on his own turf, the pussy in Jared came out. Niggas got searched before they were allowed in any of his houses and so far it had worked out in their favor. If a muthafucka wanted to try they luck, they knew they better tell the family to get out their black suits because they would find themselves six feet deep. Everyone knew that when one gun popped off, several more would follow so it was best to mind the rules of Nahvi and Meek's territory.

Nahvi collected the earnings for the night and then left the trap house with a lot of shit on his mind. He wanted so bad to get out of the lifestyle, but it seemed the closer he got, the further away his future looked. At that moment, it didn't look too bright. He really didn't want to go home because he knew he would feel empty but after driving around for another hour, he was spent. He pulled into his driveway and sat for a minute because he didn't want to rush to face his lonely world. He decided that he would get some rest and then wake up the next day with a new frame of mind. He would also call his realtor and find himself a smaller place because it felt as if he would be alone forever.

Nahvi had the heart of a hustler so he couldn't understand how he had let it get broken. He was supposed to be stronger than that and vowed that he would never open it to another woman again. He decided to take a quick shower so he could wash away the filthiness from his day. The hot water eased his mind and relaxed his soul and brought him some much needed peace. He felt like he could stay in there all night until the sound at his door brought him back to reality.

"The fuck is at my door this late? Better not be Monica's fuck ass." He chimed out loud to himself as he wrapped a towel around his most private parts and shut the shower water off. Whoever was there was determined and he swore to himself that if it was Meek, he was going to curse him the hell out. He didn't need another nigga sweating his dick that time of night. When Nahvi reached his doo, he didn't even bother to check and see who it was. He pulled it open with all his might and saw someone he didn't expect to see ever again.

Corey Robinson

Chapter Fifteen

Ashley had enough of the bullshit that was going on between her and Nahvi. Surely, they were adults and could handle what had happened better than what they did. She couldn't stand to be away from him any longer and dammit she didn't care what he said, she was going over there and fixing it. She couldn't believe that she had fallen for him so hard and so fast. There was no denying that she had love in her heart that he had placed there and no matter how hard she tried, it wasn't going away. She had been miserable without him and didn't even care if he never got out of the dope game as long as he was a part of her life.

She knew that he was home because his Denali was sitting in the driveway. She just hoped that he was alone and if he wasn't, well she'd handle that then, but she wasn't leaving until they came to an understanding and made up. Nahvi was her man and she'd be damned if she let another bitch take him, especially one who didn't appreciate him. She got out of the car and walked slowly against the night breeze and froze up when she got to the door. "Come on, Ash. you can do this." She prayed that he didn't turn her away and then knocked loudly on the polished wood.

She knocked for what seemed like forever and had almost given up but just as she was about to walk away, she heard the latch unlock.

When she turned back around, she almost lost her breath. Nahvi stood in front of her in nothing but a towel and beads of water covering his flesh. She was speechless and could feel the wetness between her legs as it began to form. She began to wonder how she had denied such a beautiful form access to her most sacred place. If anyone deserved to be inside of her, it was him and she would deny him no longer. She didn't even ask him if he was alone because honestly she didn't give a damn. She was going to have him that night even if she had to beat a bitches ass to get him.

She wasn't going to ask for permission either because this man belonged to her. She stared deep in his golden brown eyes and lost all composure. She couldn't take it anymore and realized that he was waiting for her to make the first move. He was much taller than she but she somehow managed to wrap her arms around his tattooed neck and pulled him in to her. When their lips met, it was like waves crashing in the ocean. Their tongues danced like it was a competition and both wanted to win the prize. She could feel the tears form in her eyes and knew that when she opened them they would fall from the joy she felt, in her heart, but she also knew that Nahvi would wipe them away with his loving hands.

She finally found the strength to break the kiss and pulled back from him so she could catch her breath. The front door still stood open, and she could feel the breeze brush against her hair. She quickly turned around and shut it and then turned back to the man who had stolen her heart. "Nahvi, I miss you baby and I can't stay away from you for another minute."

He looked down into her saddened eyes and then wiped away the tear that fell and made a small trail down her cheek. "I miss you too. I'm sorry I jumped to conclusions about Kelvin, and I know that I should have let you explain but …"

She stopped his words with her mouth and kissed him again. She didn't need an explanation because no matter what he said, she knew that she would forgive him. "Baby, you don't have to tell me anything. It's okay. I just can't be without you anymore and I can't wait for you to make love to me either. I'm ready, Nahvi. I'm ready to give all of myself to you."

"What? Are you sure, because I can wait on you for however long you need. I love you just that much."

Ashley didn't respond but instead pulled the towel from around his waist and grabbed a hold of what she wanted. His thickness was too large for her small hand, but she worked it anyway and with each stroke it seemed to grow even more. Ashley wasn't a quitter so she kept going. All of it belonged to her and she was going to tame that beast. She moved up and down his length with precision as she pulled one of his man nipples between her lips. When she let it go, he bent and pulled her into his arms and lifted her. He carried her to the bedroom that he had once shared with Monica but before he lied her on the bed, he asked, "Are you okay with doing this in here? I don't want you to feel disrespected or anything."

"Nahvi, I don't care where we are, as long as I'm with you."

With that being said, Nahvi placed her gently on the bed and pulled her shirt and bra off first. The pinkness of her nipples intrigued him, and he couldn't wait to have one in his mouth. His dick still stood at attention and before Ashley laid back, she took a moment to lick the precum off the head of his manhood. When she lied back, he reached down and pulled off her jeans and blue lace panties. They were his favorite pair now and any that she wore after that wouldn't mean much.

He had never been intimate with a white woman before, but he knew it couldn't have been much different. He spread her legs and the folds of her pussy opened right on up and he wasted no time putting his face where his dick would soon follow. He inhaled her scent and licked her inner thighs because he wanted to take his time with her. He had fucked a lot of bitches, but he would make thug love to her. Ashley inhaled a deep breath when he pulled her swollen clit into his warm mouth. He sucked on it gently and made her go crazy.

Slowly, he inserted a finger and could feel her tightness letting him know that she really hadn't been touched in a while. It felt good that she would allow him to be the first in a long time.

"Oh Nahvi, baby, it feels so good. You're gonna make me cum if yo don't stop."

Ashley put her hands on the back of his head because she didn't even want him to think about stopping. She'd had been given head before but it had never felt like this. She felt as if the room was spinning and she couldn't stop it no matter how hard she tried.

"Yes, Nahvi, oh baby yes. Yes."

When Ashley came, Nahvi didn't stop until her legs stopped shaking. He wanted to make sure he got every single drop of her sweetness because it was too valuable to waste. When she finished cumming, he towered over her and looked down at her flesh. He admired each and every curve and wondered how he had gotten so lucky to have her as his. He got all the way in the bed and positioned himself between her legs. He didn't want to hurt her, so he took his time entering her body. He got lost in ecstasy once the head of his dick pushed through her opening. The tightness wrapped around him like a snake that wrapped its body around its prey. He knew that he wouldn't be able to hang too long at first because she would make that first nut come out quickly but after that she would be in for a rude awakening. The wetness of her walls made Nahvi's knees go weak and as his balls hit her ass cheeks he knew that he would ever give it to another. His dick belonged to Ashley and no other woman alive would be able to satisfy him.

"Damn baby, this pussy good. You gon' make a nigga come too soon."

She looked up at him, smiled and enjoyed the pleasure he brought her. She'd had plenty of dick but none that felt so good. She could see herself getting all that good dick for the rest of her life because she knew that she would never get tired of having Nahvi inside of her. She reached her hands around his back and clenched his ass cheeks because when he came she didn't want him to pull out of her. She wanted each and every drop of him inside of her.

"Ash, baby I'm 'bout to cum."

No sooner than he said it, she felt him release all of his seed and fill her up. The thought of one day having his children crossed her mind and made her heart fill with even more love. When he had filled her completely, he looked into her eyes and said the words she had longed to hear but in his own thuggish way.

"You know a nigga loves you right?"

"I know baby, I know."

The two lovers shared a moment of silence and just looked in the glory of what they were feeling. They had been apart for too long and wanted to savor every moment. Nahvi felt a little embarrassed because he'd came so quickly but he couldn't help himself. Ashley felt just that good, but he knew that he would make it up on the next round because he wasn't quite through with her yet. He wanted to feel her tightness around his manhood again. Hell, he needed to feel it to be complete. Where had she been all of his life?

"Ash, look. That day you came and saw Monica leaving here, nothing happened between us. I hope yo know that a nigga respects you more than that. Even when I'm mad."

"Oh Nahvi, I know and it's okay because that shit is in the past. Let's just worry about our future now." She ran her hand along his cheek and then kissed those perfectly formed lips. She wished that they could stay right there and hold each other forever but reality set in when she heard Nahvi's stomach talking. Grrrrr.

They shared a laugh and Nahvi rolled off of her onto his back. "Looks like I'm hungry for more than pussy."

"Uh, yeah and I think I need to get up and feed my man before I come back in here and put him to sleep."

"Oh yeah, you think you going to wear me out? I think it's gonna be you that taps out first. Cause a nigga like me be putting down that good loving and you know you ass can't hang."

"Yeah, we'll see about that."

Nahvi's stomach growled again from the appetite he had worked up, plus he hadn't been eating right since they had been apart. He was sure that Ashley needed to eat too but he had still not filled his kitchen with the things he needed.

"Aye, I'll tell you what. You stay your pretty ass right here and I'm gonna run down to the IHOP and get us something hot to eat and then I'm gonna finish what you started and couldn't."

"Oh, well keep talking that shit and I'm gonna show you how a real woman gets down."

Ashley and Nahvi shared another kiss before he got up and put some clothes on. She couldn't take her eyes off of him and watch his every move. Damn he was fine, and he belonged to her. She didn't want to spend one second away from him, so she asked, "Babe, do you want me to ride with you? I don't know if I'm going to be able to handle you being away from me."

He leaned over and kissed her and then slid on his Timbs and answered, "Nah, you stay just like that because as soon as I'm done eating, I'm coming for dessert."

With that being said, Nahvi grabbed some cash and his keys and walked out to the night breeze not knowing that it would be a minute before he walked back in.

Chapter Sixteen

Nahvi pulled into the IHOP and walked inside with thoughts of Ashley still on his mind. He never noticed the dark black Buick with tinted windows pull in behind him and park. He purchased two breakfast platters and two orange juices. He had never been a man that liked coffee, but he got a cup for Ashley just in case it was her thing. He paid the cashier and walked out without a care in the world. He walked to the passenger side first and put the food, drinks down in the seat and then walked to the driver's side. His dick throbbed from the thought of being inside his woman again. He decided that he would fuck her so good and so long she'd be bedridden for a week. He smiled at the thought and stuck his key in the ignition. As soon as he put his truck in reverse, a knock came at the window. When he turned his head to see who had disturbed him, he saw the badge.

"What the hell is going on? This has got to be some sort of fucking joke." He mumbled quietly to himself.

Nahvi rolled down his window and listened to the words that left the officers mouth.

"JaNahvi Karter, I need you to step out of the vehicle. You're under arrest for the assault of Kelvin Brown."

"What the hell did you just say? I know that pussy muthafucka did not put the fucking police on me." Nahvi could not believe his luck. He knew that he was wrong when he punched Kelvin in the parking lot of the 7-Eleven but he never would have expected him to put his boys on the force on his ass. That was a move that only a fuck boy would pull and he would make sure Kelvin's ass paid.

"Mr. Karter, I'm gonna need you to step out of the vehicle real slow with your hands up. Please don't make me tell you again."

He cut off his engine and stepped out slowly just like the officer told him to do because he didn't want to end up being another statistic at the hands of the police. He had known that Kelvin and his crew had the cracker on their side from the last encounter he'd had with them that put him away for eight years. He thought about Ashley and wondered if she would wait for him because he felt in his heart that he was about to be gone a long ass time.

"Aye man, can I at least call my girl so she can come pick up my ride?" Nahvi asked as the officer placed the cuffs around his wrists.

"You'll get your phone call at the station, Mr. Karter. In the meantime, I suggest you use this opportunity to remain silent."

"Man fuck that. Y'all fucking crackers think Kelvin Brown's ass won't turn on y'all then you dumb as hell. His bitch ass should have come to see me himself. Pussy ass muthafucka. We could have handled this like two grown ass men instead of this petty ass bullshit. Fuckin' snitch ass bitch ass muthafucka."

Nahvi continued to curse all the way to the station, with the officer continuously looking back at him and shaking his head. Nahvi didn't stop selling out until they pulled up in the booking garage at the station. He was more than ready to get the cuff's off of his wrist and call Ashley. He knew that she had to be worried by now. The officer put him in a holding cell and removed the cuff's and then walked away without saying a word.

"Yo man, what the fuck? What about my phone call!" Nahvi hollered out, but no one acknowledged his presence. He decided to sit down and wait until someone came to process him and then he would call her. He put his elbows on his knees and his hands in a praying position and thought about those eight years he'd spent before. He hadn't even been out two years yet and there he was already back in. He knew how the system worked and he didn't stand a chance against some crooked ass police. He remembered when he was in the streets running shit real heavy. His right hand had told him that he needed to put one of the boys in blue on his payroll, but Nahvi couldn't see himself selling out like that and giving any of his power to the pigs. To him, that was a bitch move. He wondered how much money Kelvin had put in the crackers pocket for him to be on his side. Did putting him away really mean that much to him?

Nahvi felt like he waited for hours before a knock sounded at the window of the cell he had been sitting in.

"Hey Karter, come on. I'm going to take you to make your phone call before we process you in and get you comfortable." The officer smiled and Nahvi knew his white ass was being sarcastic, but he didn't have time for those little boy games.

"Man, suck my dick."

"Oh, don't worry Mr. Karter, I'm sure they'll all be lined up to get a piece of you."

Nahvi wanted to haul off and punch the officer in the face but his fist was what had got him there in the first place, so he thought better of it. All he wanted was to hear Ashley's voice and know that she was alright. He got to the phone and punched in the numbers quickly and breathed a sigh of relief when she answered.

"Nahvi, where the hell are you at? Are you okay? I've been worried sick about you."

He braced himself and told her what had went down, "Look I'm down at the jail. Kelvin's fuck ass had me booked for assault. My truck's still at the IHOP and I need you to go pick it up for me and then call Meek to get me the lawyer."

"Nahvi, what are you talking about? How could Kelvin get you locked up when you haven't done anything to him?"

He never told her about the altercation between him and Kelvin. He just didn't think it would matter. He would have rather faced bloodshed than be locked away from the woman he loved and not being able to protect her. "Look, Ash. I ran into his fuck ass at the store, and I just couldn't help myself. I laid him the fuck out and his pussy ass called the fucking pigs on me. I'm sorry, but my mind was fucked up because I thought I had lost you and that shit was eating me up inside."

"Oh, Nahvi. What were you thinking? Look, do you have a bond or anything? I'm coming to get you."

"Save your trip because if they do give me a bond it won't be until after I see the judge on Monday. In the meantime, I need you to call Meek. He should have us a lawyer on standby and make sure you go pick up my ride."

"Okay babe and Nahvi, don't worry. I'm a stick by you every step of the way. I love you."

"Aye, I gotta go, but I love you too and no matter what happens, don't ever forget that."

Nahvi hung up the pay phone with a heavy load in his heart, but he knew he had to be strong for Ashley's sake. Even though he was the one locked up. She would need him more than ever. The guard walked him to the processing area where he was photographed and fingerprinted and then he was taken to another cell. He didn't even bother making the bed because he just didn't have it in him. He threw the worn blanket over the bare mattress and as soon as his head hit the soiled plastic of the pillow, he was out.

Chapter Seventeen

Ashley's heart broke when Nahvi called and gave her the news of his incarceration. She couldn't believe that Kelvin had the audacity to put his people on him and take him to jail. She knew that he was only doing it to hurt her because for some reason, he enjoyed it. She got dressed in a hurry and then called Meek who answered on the first ring.

"Sup Ash, if you looking for ya girl she ain't got the strength to talk right now. Ya know your boy put it on her ass."

"Thanks for the information but I did not want to hear that. I'm actually calling because I need you to come get me and take me to pick up Nahvi's truck. He's in jail, Meek and he said to tell you to contact the lawyer for him."

"The fuck you mean he's in jail? How the hell did that shit happen?"

"Well, it seems that Kelvin had him booked on an assault charge for busting him in the mouth. He said he won't get a bond until Monday. What am I gonna do, Meek? We just made up. I can't lose him again."

Ashley could feel the tears as they formed in her eyes. She knew she needed to be strong but how could she when all her strength had been locked up.

"Look, don't worry about my boy. I got the best lawyer in the state on payroll and he'll get Nahvi out of there. You gon' be alright, Ash. I'm gonna make sure of it. Give me a minute to get dressed and I'll be there to get you."

Meek didn't give her a chance to say anything back before he hung up. She just couldn't believe that this was happening. There was no way she'd let Kelvin get away with what he'd done, and she vowed that as soon as she picked up Nahvi's truck, she would go pay him a visit. She paced the floor for what seemed like forever until she finally heard Meek pull up.

Ashley didn't even give him a chance to alert her of his arrival before she was out the door. She jumped in his ride and seen that Tracey wasn't with him. In a way, she was glad because she didn't want her best friend involved in the bullshit going on in her life. She knew that Tracey would have her back at all costs but to pull her into a war would have been dead wrong.

"What did you do with Tracey?" She asked him breaking the silence between them.

"I left her at my crib so she could get some rest because she's gonna need it fuckin with me."

"Damn Meek, you got my girl like that already? I know one thing, if you break her heart, I'm a fuck you up myself."

"Nah ma, she's in good hands. We just having a little fun right now but I'm feeling her for real. You ain't got shit to worry about, and that goes both ways. Don't worry 'bout that nigga Kelvin because he gon' get served for the bullshit he did to my boy. I give you my word on that."

Ashley didn't want Meek to get fucked up behind Kelvin either, but she knew how the streets got down. You fuck with one person one the crew, you fuckin with them all. There was nothing she could do because Kelvin had dug his grave and if Meek made him lie in it, then so be it. She would still make the trip to see him although, deep in her heart, she knew that she should stay away. Kelvin had never meant her any good but doing what he did to Nahvi topped everything else in the past.

"I'm glad that you and my boy worked that shit out. I ain't never seen him act like that over no female so I know he feeling you deep. My nigga good people and that bitch Monica ain't shit so don't ever let that mufucka see you sweat. He saw her true colors and everything he had for her faded away the first day he met you."

Ashley smiled at the words Meek had spit at her. It felt good to hear them especially coming from his friend because it showed her that Nahvi would never hide how he felt for her. Meek pulled into the parking lot of the IHOP and asked, "Hey, you need me to follow you home?"

"No Meek, I'll be good from here. I'm a big girl. Please let me know what the lawyer says, and I'll let you know if I hear from Nahvi again. Thanks, okay."

"No problem. I fuck with you the long way. Now if you'll excuse me, I got to get back to ya girl."

"Alright Meek. Tell Tracey I'll call her tomorrow."

Ashley had brought the spare keys to Nahvi's ride and got in. The first thing she noticed was the two breakfast trays and the three drink cups in the passenger seat. Until she saw them, she had forgotten that she hadn't eaten. The aroma of the food made her stomach growl, so she decided to warm one of the platters up when she got back to Nahvi's. She didn't want to return to her place because being in his condo made her feel closer to him. Just as she was about to back out of the parking spot, Kelvin's pearl white E-Class Mercedes blocked her path.

"I swear that this bastard is going to get himself killed fucking with me," she said as she watched him get out of his car and walk up to the door of where she sat. She didn't bother rolling down the window because when she cursed his ass out she wanted to look in his eyes and let him know that she meant every word.

Ashley opened the door and got out to face the man she had once given her all to but for some reason, he seemed taller than usual. She felt like David about to fight Goliath with nothing but a slingshot and a stone but unlike David, her only weapon was her words and she hoped that they would be enough.

"You motherfucker. How in the hell could yo do some shit like that to Nahvi. You and your childish ass games are getting old, Kelvin. You should have handled that shit like a real man, but I see that deep down, you really are a pussy."

She felt his hand even after it contacted her face. The stinging sensation felt like needles were being stuck into her flesh. She rubbed her cheek and looked at him like he had lost his mind. All that time they were together, he had never so much as raised a hand to her. As many times as he'd broken her heart, a blow to the face may have felt better.

"You must have forgotten who the fuck you are talking to. Your ass think because you fucking a big dawg like JaNahvi Karter that you way up on the totem pole now. Bitch, I'm about to put your ass back down to size."

She could not believe the words he spat at her and it caused her soul to rumble. "Kelvin, what did I ever do to you to make you treat me this way? I don't understand. You cheated on me the entire time we were together. You even had two babies on me. I forgave you and still stuck it in there with you. I just can't figure out why you don't want me to be happy. Nahvi is good to me. Way better than you ever were. Please Kelvin, I know somewhere deep inside that cold heart of yours, there has to be some kind of warmth and compassion."

Kelvin looked at her like he really cared about what she said but she knew him like no other and he didn't break that easily. His heart was too cold, and his mind was hard to change. He had the mentality that what was once his would always be his.

"So, you want a nigga to let you walk around here and play house with the fucking enemy? You know the code of the streets and that shit ain't gon' fly with me. You gonna always be mine. You better go somewhere and find you a square ass muthafucka with that shit you talking.

"Kelvin, you walking around harboring a ten year old beef ain't cool. Nahvi paid for what he done, and he's moved on. Why can't you just do the same?"

"His ass should have thought about that before he put his hands on me."

"So, you put the police on him. Don't y'all have a street code for snitching? That's fucked up, Kelvin. I don't have shit else to say to you. Stay the hell away from me and Nahvi. I'm with him now and no matter how hard you come at us, you can't break what we have built. Goodbye, Kelvin."

Ashley turned around and got back in the truck, she'd heard enough and knew that no matter what she said, there was just no getting through to him. Whatever consequences he faced would be solely on him because after what he did to Nahvi, she knew his crew was going to step up. It was just how the trenches rolled.

Kelvin stood by the truck and stared at her through soulless eyes. It made her skin crawl in ways it never had before.

She started the Denali and put it in reverse, but Kelvin still didn't move. She wasn't beyond moving his car for him, but she just didn't want to make things worse. She gave him one final glance and then he walked back to his car, got in, and sped off.

Ashley backed out of the parking lot with ease and right when she was about to pull out, a black suburban rammed into the side of the Denali. She didn't have a chance to see who it was because it came out of nowhere. It felt like her ribs were broken and made it hard for her to move but somehow she had to find the strength. Nahvi needed her and she needed him. When the back of the truck caught on fire, Ashley found a way to crawl over the console and out of the passenger door. There was no way she could have gotten out of the driver's side door because it was smashed all the way in. The pain shot through her body with every move she made but still, she managed to push through. She thought of Nahvi and wondered if the hit had been meant for him and if so, she was thankful that it had been her instead.

She loved him so much she would give her life for his because without him, she wouldn't have much of one. She couldn't understand why no one had showed up to help her but she hoped they would soon. She wasn't ready to die and prayed that God would spare her. She had so much more to share with Nahvi before she left the earth. She could see people begin to gather around where she had crawled to and laid down, and right after she heard the sounds of the sirens, everything went black.

Chapter Eighteen

"Good job, baby. You know a nigga gonna fuck you real proper for that shit."

"Mmm, and a bitch can't wait."

Monica had slid Kelvin her phone number. One night when he had went by Tonya's to see his son. Tonya hadn't been home at the time and as always Kelvin Junior was left in her care. When he showed up looking for Tonya, Monica opened the door with only a short T-shirt and some thongs on. He didn't know this, but Monica had did it intentionally. Shit, she needed some dick and from what she'd heard, Kelvin knew how to lay it down.

"Sup, Monica? Where Tonya ass at? I'm trying to spend some time with my shorty."

"She ain't here, Kelvin and I don't know when she'll be back but Junior's in the room sleep. You more than welcome to come in and wake him up."

Kelvin looked Monica up and down from her freshly braided micros to her long caramel toned legs. He had always been a foot man so when he got down to her pretty manicured toes, he grabbed his dick and said, "Oh yeah, well it looks like one Junior has already been woke up. What's up with you?"

Monica looked at Kelvin sideways, but she took an extra minute and analyzed his whole being. His corn rows were braided into a perfect design and the one carat diamonds in each ear set it off even more. His deep brown eyes looked mysterious, and she wondered just what he had in his soul that she could explore. The goatee that outlined his lips and jawline made a bitch want to edge it with her pussy. Kelvin rocked a wife beater that showed off his toned muscles with tattoos that covered every inch of skin on his arms. When her eyes traveled a little further down, she could see the dick print as it tried to push through the beige Dickey khaki's that he wore. His white shell toed Nikes made her pussy wet. When she trailed her eyes back up to him, she finally found the courage to speak.

"Now you know that Tonya is my friend, Kelvin and a bitch would be dead wrong to chill with you like that so if you want to come in and spend some time with your son then you're more than welcome but ain't shit else about to go down in here."

Kelvin smiled and stepped inside. He knew that Monica was just talking shit because he hadn't met a bitch alive that he couldn't fuck, and she would be no exception. He stood in front of her so close she could feel his breath upon her throat. When she swallowed hard and shut her eyes, he reached under the T-shirt and rubbed on her panties. He could feel her swollen clit through the fabric and when he went down a little further, he felt the wetness that she had released.

"You might as well go ahead and let me take care of that for you."

Monica couldn't find the words to deny him. When he pulled the crotch of the thongs to the side and slid a long slender finger into her wetness, she couldn't stop him. When he pulled his finger out, he put it in her mouth and made her suck the juices off. Then, he stuck his finger back inside of her and after sliding it in and out a few times, she came. When he pulled it back out, he put it in his own mouth and stated, "Damn, this pussy nice and sweet. I don't know how that nigga walked away from this."

Monica knew that she should stop while she was still ahead but something inside her prevented it. Kelvin grabbed the bottom of her T-shirt and pulled it from over her head. Her breasts weren't very big, but they were a handful and to Kelvin, anything more than that would have been a waste. Her dark brown areolas encircled her long plump nipples, and he couldn't help but lean down and pull one into his mouth.

Monica felt like she was about to faint from the feeling he was giving her. The last piece of dick she had was from Jared and although his dope boy finesses turned her on and his pockets were long as fuck, he lacked in the dick department. She had barely felt him inside of her, so she never left his presence satisfied. She knew from the print in Kelvin's pants that he was about to touch her ribcage and she couldn't wait.

"Uh Kelvin, damn that feels so good, but I think we should stop."

Kelvin ignored her pleas but made her continue to moan. "Let's go over here to the couch and get them panties off you. I'm a show you how a real nigga is supposed to make you feel."

When Monica turned around to do as he said he walked close behind her and undid his jeans on the way. "Just go head and bend that ass over. Let me put some hardness in ya life."

When she bent over and held on to the back of the couch, Kelvin spread her open and pushed deep inside of her. Her pussy was wet and tight and made Kelvin's knees buckle from under him.

"Damn Moni, I should've been hit this pussy. Shit so damn good you make a nigga want to plant some seeds."

Monica heard what he said but couldn't find the word to tell him that if he planted some babies inside of her, she wasn't going to keep the little bastards. She refused to let a crumb snatcher fuck up her body. A baby had never been in her plans. She told herself that she would make an appointment for the next week to go and get a depo shot so Kelvin could cream her walls as often as he wanted, and she wouldn't suffer any repercussions.

"Yeah Kelvin, go ahead nigga. Push that cum all up inside of me, but whatever you do don't pull that big muthafucka out."

"Yeah, you like this dick, Moni. You can ride this mufucka anytime you want. This dick is yours now." He exclaimed as sweat rolled down his forehead.

Monica knew that he was lying because Kelvin was too much of a Casanova to fuck just one bitch, but she didn't care if he said words to her that he didn't mean. She knew it was just the dick talking and as long as it talked to her pussy, she would listen.

"I'm 'bout to cum, Moni. I'm 'bout to empty all these babies inside of you. Shit."

Monica enjoyed the feeling of his nut sack hitting her clit as they swung with each thrust, but when he pushed a thumb in her back hole it made her cum instantly. A few seconds later, Kelvin gripped her ass cheeks real tight and thrust inside of her one more time. He stood behind her with his ass cheeks and thigh muscles clenched tightly and emptied out all he had. When he pulled out of Monica, she turned around and pulled his semi hard dick into her mouth and cleaned it off with her tongue.

From that moment on, Monica and Kelvin would fuck every chance they got so it came as no surprise when Monica agreed to help him get at Nahvi and Ashley. That white bitch had ruined her happy home, at least in Monica's mind. She would enjoy paying Nahvi back for dissing her.

They had it all set up. Kelvin knew that when Nahvi finally came out of the house, he wouldn't be expecting the police to run up on him. Kelvin had one of his boys stand watch down from Nahvi's condo one night when he knew that Ashley was there. He told him that as soon as he saw Nahvi come out alone to call him and when he did, Kelvin texted the dirty cop that was on his payroll.

Once Nahvi was hauled off, Kelvin and Monica knew that he'd call Ashley to pick up his truck and when she came, the rest would be history. Kelvin told Monica to only hit the Denali lightly, but she'd be damned if she gave that bitch a chance to walk away unscathed. The Suburban barely had a dent in it but Kelvin had it taken to the chop shop so no one could ever identify it. She was happy about making Kelvin proud and decided that she would no longer hide her romance with him from Tonya.

She was sitting in front of the television painting her toenails Kelvin's favorite color when Tonya came in from her rendezvous. She was tired of her coming in and flaunting all the shit that random niggas spent they money on. Monica had been enjoying her time with Kelvin when Tonya would be out but the fact that he hadn't spent no major paper on her made her feel some type of way. She was giving him the pussy but all she got in return was the dick and although it was good, it just wasn't enough anymore.

"Bitch, did you hear about Nahvi getting knocked and his girl being laid up in a hospital bed?"

Monica rolled her eyes because, of course she knew. "That is old news, Tonya. It happened like what, two days ago? That nigga will bond out tomorrow because them crackers can't keep a man like him down."

"Well, you seem to be acting like it don't bother you."

Monica smiled at Tonya and her friend knew just what that meant. Only some good dick could make a bitch smile so hard. Tonya wanted to know everything too. "No. Bitch, you been getting some good dick from somewhere and your ass ain't tell me. Do I know him?"

Monica knew that her time to shine had finally came so she held nothing back. "Well don't be mad but Kelvin's been stopping by while you're out, and things have progressed between us."

"Hold up bitch, I know you ain't sitting in my living room fucking my son's father. You playing with me right?"

"Do I look like I'm playing? You ain't giving it up to him. Besides, y'all ain't even together like that no more."

"How the hell could you do some foul shit like that Monica. You're supposed to be my fucking friend and yet you fucking my man."

"Kelvin is not your man. The only ties you have to him is that little bastard you keep leaving me with. Shit, it's almost like I'm his momma."

The slap came before Monica could block it. She couldn't believe that Tonya had put her hands on her. She knew that telling her about what had been going on would piss her off, but the slap was unexpected.

"Bitch, I want you out of my shit right now and stay the hell away from Kelvin."

"Fuck you, I don't need your ass and as far as Kelvin goes, that's where you'll find me."

"Oh yeah, well I guess you don't know him at all. Let me know how that goes for you!"

Monica ran in the room and gathered her belongings. However, there was no way she'd be able to carry all of it with her so she called Kelvin to see if he would come to get her. She was disappointed when her call was sent to voicemail, so she sent him a text, but little did she know, Kelvin was too busy to read it. When Monica turned around she saw Tonya as she stood at the door with her arms crossed over her chest. She watched Monica so hard it made her uncomfortable.

"Are you just gonna stand there and watch me?"

"Bitch, you went behind my back and fucked Kelvin, so I don't know what else you're capable of doing."

"Fuck you, Tonya. If you would have been doing more than spending his money, I couldn't have slid in so that's your bad."

"Yeah, and just how much does he spend on you?" Tonya asked and waited for Monica's response, but none ever came so she added, "That's what I thought."

Monica ignored the question because she was embarrassed to say that Kelvin had hardly spent one dime on her. "Look, I got to leave some of my things here, but I'll be back to get them."

"Nah you take that shit with you because whatever you leave is going in the trash which is actually where you belong."

"Alright, alright." Monica exclaimed and only packed her most important items because she knew that Tonya was serious. She pulled out her phone once again, only that time she called on Uber to come pick her up. Tonya made her wait outside although it was raining and by the time the driver got to her, she was soaking wet.

"Bout damn time," she said to the driver when he finally pulled up. She did a double take when he got close enough to pick up her things. He was young but she could tell he had his shit together. When he caught her staring, he smiled but when she remembered that a man was the reason she was standing out in the rain, she gave him Kelvin's address and got in the minivan.

The ride to Kelvin's was quiet but Monica enjoyed the little peace of mind. She continued to look at her phone and hoped that Kelvin would eventually text her and tell her he had her back, but that text never came. When the driver pulled up to Kelvin's place he got out and helped her get her baggage out, "Have a nice night ma'am." She smiled and thanked him and then picked her bags up. Kelvin had never told her where he lived but Monica was the type of bitch that could find out anything she wanted. She knew that Kelvin would be surprised to see her because they hadn't made plans for that night. Monica looked around and was amazed by how Kelvin was living. His house was huge with a three car garage and nicely manicured lawn. She wondered what the inside held and couldn't wait to find out. She rang the doorbell and waited. Her heart began to pound faster thinking that no one was going to answer.

"Come on, Kelvin, please answer," she pleaded because she had nowhere else to go. Right when she pulled out her phone and started to dial Kelvin's number again, lights began to come on in the house. "Yes, it's about time."

When the door opened, Monica gasped because it wasn't who she expected. "Who in the hell are you and where is Kelvin at?"

In a calm nonchalant voice, the female that stared back at her exclaimed, "I'm Brandy and Kelvin is upstairs in our bedroom but you're more than welcome to come in."

The smile Brandy had on her face pissed Monica off, but she still walked inside. She wanted to know what the fuck was going on with her new man. No sooner than she stepped in the door, she heard Kelvin's voice, "Baby who is that at the door?" But before Brandy had a chance to answer him, he noticed Monica standing at the bottom of the stairs.

"The fuck is you doing at my house?"

Monica looked at Kelvin with a deep hatred in her eyes. "You motherfucker. You up in this big ass house with another bitch but fucking me. You better tell this hoe just who the hell I am."

Brandy slammed the front door and walked up to Monica with a fire in her eyes that would burn through even the thickest glass and respond to what Monica had said, but she looked up at Kelvin first. "It's okay baby, I'll take care of this for you," and then she turned back to Monica. "He doesn't have to tell me who you are bitch because I already know. As a matter of fact, I know about every bitch he fucks. Do you think I'm worried? Hell no. Kelvin comes home to me at night so whatever you thought you and him had, is not. Now if you'll excuse us, we were in the middle of something." Brandy walked up the stairs and stopped when she got to Kelvin. She put her arm around him and then tiptoed up to kiss him. She untied the robe he had on and then reached down and wrapped her manicured fingers around his manhood. She stroked it a couple of times and then stated, "I'll be in the bed waiting for you, baby. Handle the light weight."

Brandy got to the top of the stairs and looked down at Monica one last time before she dropped the robe she wore and revealed her toned naked body. She smiled at Monica, blew her a kiss, and walked away.

Kelvin didn't even bother tying his robe back up. Hell, Monica had already seen the dick plenty of times. Wasn't no use in hiding it now. He walked down to where she stood at the bottom of the stairs and took her last bit of dignity. "Look Monica, you just a wet pussy to me like the rest of them bitches. Don't you ever bring your ass out looking for me again. When I feel like I want to see you, I'll find you. Don't ever disrespect my woman like this again." He walked to the front door, opened it, and then turned back to Monica, "Get the hell out of our home. I'll get up with you later."

Monica picked up her bags and proceeded to walk back out but before she did she made sure that Kelvin felt her pain, "You are a piece of shit. I fucked up my friendship by fooling around with you and now, I don't have anywhere to go. I will tell you this though. Your ass is going to pay for this so I suggest you watch you back. You ain't seen the last of me." Then she walked out.

Chapter Nineteen

"Aye yo' my nigga, why the hell Ash ain't answering her phone? I done called like ten times."

Nahvi had been trying to call Ashley all day, but she never answered her phone. He didn't want to think the worst and believe that she had dissed him so soon like many others did. The last time he was locked up, but he didn't know what else to think at that moment. Head already talked to the lawyer and knew that he would be getting released the next morning. Her face was the first one he wanted to see when he walked out.

Meek hated to tell Nahvi the news about what happened, especially when he was already going through other shit, but he really had no other choice. "Nahvi, you good up in there? I'll be there first thing tomorrow to scoop you up."

"Nah man, I'm trying to see my girl but looks like her ass done got ghost on me. The fuck is up with that?"

"Look, I wasn't trying to give you any bad news on top of the shit you going through but ya girl laid up in the hospital."

"What? Man, what the hell happened? Is she alright? Nigga, quit beating around the bush and fill my ass in." Nahvi felt like his heart would fall completely out of his chest. Ashley was his everything and to find out something had happened to her fucked him up really bad.

"She good man. She was pulling out of the IHOP with your truck and a fucking Suburban came out of nowhere and hit the driver side. She had to climb out to the passenger door because your shit caught fire. She got a few broken ribs and some bruises and scratches but other than that, she gon' be alright. They wanted to keep her for a couple of days under observation but they letting her go tomorrow, so you gon' be picking her ass up instead."

"Nigga, that story don't sound right to me. I'm a put my life on that. The Suburban ain't just come from nowhere. I feel like a fucka sent it and if I find out my feelings are right, a bitch gonna have to see me."

"Don't worry dawg, I already got my feelers out. We gon' get to the bottom of it and you know if we find out it was intentional, people gonna have to see us."

"Damn right they are. Aye man, stop by and check on my girl. Tell her I love her, and I'll see her tomorrow."

"You know I got you, my boy. See ya tomorrow."

Nahvi hung up the phone and held his head down. He was pissed that he wasn't out there to keep Ashley out of harm's way. He felt in his heart that the accident wasn't no accident after all. Somebody was going to pay for what happened to the woman he had fallen in love with.

"Aye yo, playa, you done with that phone? I need to call my girl."

Nahvi heard the dude behind him ask and only then did he realize that he was still standing in front of the phone. He looked at him and moved away from the phone. He went and sat on his bunk and thought about his mother. She would have been disappointed if she would have seen the way his life had been lived. She always used to tell him that the streets were no good. He could still hear her voice, "JaNahvi, I want you to stay out of them streets because they ain't nothing but trouble. You finish school and go on to college so you can get you a good decent job and be somebody."

She had so many high hopes for him but when she died, her hopes died with her because without her guidance, Nahvi had to do what he needed to make sure he was okay. He had become a product of the streets because he'd be damned if he let the foster system suck him in. He managed to dodge a sign of relief the day he turned eighteen. He made his impact in the streets and the rest was history. He was a respected young dealer who didn't mind sharing his wealth. He knew that being greedy could get a muthafucka killed. He felt like there was enough for everyone to eat off the same plate.

With all the money and hood fame, came the women who all wanted a piece of the young thug. When Nahvi got his first piece of pussy, he felt like he was on top of the world. One piece of pussy led to many more. He made sure to always wear protection, another thing that his momma instilled in him. She always told him that if he wasn't ready to take care of a bunch of children then he needed to make sure he didn't produce any children. Plus, he had luckily never caught any diseases. He was on top of his game when the enemies started rearing their ugly faces. A few years later, he caught the assault case that sent him away for eight long years and now Nahvi found himself back inside a place he said he'd never go to again. He couldn't believe that he'd fucked up like that. He let his anger take control of him. He was just thankful he wasn't going back to prison for it.

He knew that he couldn't sit there and dwell on old shit all night so Nahvi laid back and shut his eyes to get himself some much needed sleep.

The sound of someone calling his name woke him from his deep slumber, "Karter, time to go. Get your ass up and let's get this over with.

"Oh shit," Nahvi could not believe that morning had come so soon. His thoughts had worn him out and he felt like he was still stuck in them. He laid there a minute not wanting to get up, but thoughts of Ashley came to his mind and willed him to move.

There was no way he'd leave there without rinsing off, so he took a quick shower and brushed his teeth. Wasn't nothing from there he wanted to keep so when he put on his clothes, he walked right out. "Them niggas can have that shit," he said to himself, and he meant it. He knew he needed to get a level head so shit like that didn't happen anymore.

After signing all the release papers, he walked out the front door and saw Meek standing beside a new silver Denali. "Nice ride, nigga. Told your ass to get one of these. Bout damn time you listened." He walked up to Meek and gave him some dap and then they embraced into a man hug. When Meek reached out and handed Nahvi a set of keys, he gave him a surprised look, "For me my nigga?"

"Did you think I'd let you walk outta there and not have you your own shit? Nigga, I ain't driving your black ass around so how the hell else you gon' get to where you need to be?"

"Thanks man. Good looking out." Nahvi admired Meek's loyalty to him. He had been a real friend and he knew that Meek would always have his back. He had no idea that when he first met him, he'd turn out to be the realest mufucka he knew.

The two men jumped in the Denali and Nahvi pulled out of the parking lot with one destination in mind. It felt like it took forever to make it to the hospital where he would pick up his queen. When he finally made it, he jumped out and ran inside. Meek had already told him what floor Ashley was on, so he knew where to find her. When he got to the floor, Ashley sat in a wheelchair at the nurse's desk looking as beautiful as ever.

"Oh my God, baby. I was about to lose my damn mind worrying about you. Are you okay?"

Nahvi wanted to embrace her, but he was too afraid that he'd hurt her, so he just kneeled down in front of her instead.

"Oh Nahvi, I'm better now. God, I missed you baby. I thought that I was going to lose you."

"Nah, a nigga going to have to kill me to keep me away from you. Ain't no way in hell I'm gon' let them crackers send me back up that road. You stuck with me girl."

The two lovers shared a laugh and then Nahvi pushed Ashley to the elevator so he could get her home. They'd been through so much in such a short amount of time and he hoped that there would be no more obstacles in his way. Nahvi dropped Meek off first and promised to get up with him in a few hours. He just needed a little time to get Ashley settled first. He decided that it would be best if he took Ashely to her own apartment instead of his condo, at least until shit was handled in the streets. He'd get with his realtor and get her to find him and Ash a nice home on the outskirts of Atlanta. His street days were coming to an end. He'd make sure his beef with Kelvin would be his last.

"Nahvi, why are you taking me to my place? I don't want to be away from you any longer."

The pleading look in her eyes broke his heart because Nahvi felt like he'd let her down already. "Look, Ash, it's only temporary. I just need to make sure you straight until I can get this nigga off my back."

"And you think I'm better off over here? Kelvin would feel more comfortable coming here but yet, this is where you want to leave me. In a fucking strike zone?"

"Baby, listen. I would kill everybody in this fucking city just to make sure you were safe. Let me handle this nigga and get back right. I'm a go to my place and get a few things and then I'll be back. I give you my word."

Ashley looked at him sadly because she knew he was about to make the streets feel his pain. She prayed that it was not the last time she saw him and got out of the truck. She didn't say not one word when she shut the door behind and walked away with more than just her bones aching. She had fallen in love with Nahvi and his pain became hers. She had to believe that God would send him back to her.

Nahvi didn't leave the parking lot until Ashley made it all the way inside of her apartment. He backed up and called Meek. "Aye dawg I'm a need you to get with ya girl and tell her to make sure Ashley stays inside."

"I can do that. Matter of fact, she right here beside me. I'll take her over there myself. What's up with you? You ready to meet up so we can go handle that shit?" Meek was anxious to put something hot in Kelvin's ass but Nahvi didn't want to move too quick and fuck it up."

"Nah, I'm 'bout to go to my crib and pick up a few things so I can go chill at my baby's place. I'll call you as soon as I'm done and then we can plan the move."

"Aiight. I'll wait for your call."

Nahvi pulled into his driveway and got out so he could get the things he needed. He just didn't feel safe bringing Ashley there anymore because that would make her an open target with nowhere to run. He needed to make sure that he protected her above all else and by any means necessary. He knew that he would one day die in the streets but now he had the will to fight. He needed more time with Ashley first.

When he walked inside his condo, he could still smell Ashley's womanly essence. It was almost as if she were still there. He went into his bedroom and packed some clothes and then jumped in the shower to freshen up. When he was done, he made sure to lock everything up. He would get his realtor to list the condo and get rid of it because once he handled his street beef, he was going to pull out and leave Meek with the reigns back in his hands. Nahvi opened his front door and ran into an unexpected visitor.

"Nahvi, I know you probably hate me, and I know you don't want shit else to do with me, but please could you just give me a minute. I have some things I need to say to you."

Nahvi let out a sign of irritation because he couldn't believe that Monica would show up at his door again after that bullshit stunt she had pulled. "Monica, I honestly don't want to hear shit you have to say. I got some place to be, and I don't have time for you fucking drama."

"Please Nahvi. Please just listen. I'm not here to cause you any more problems.

"What the hell do you want? I'll give you two minutes to speak your peace."

"Can we go inside?"

"Hell nah. I remember what happened the last time your ass went inside. That shit ain't gonna happen."

"Nahvi, I'm serious when I say I'm not bringing you no bullshit. I need to talk to you about Kelvin Brown."

Nahvi looked at Monica sideways because he wondered why the fuck she would come to him about Kelvin but then he remembered that she was a nosy bitch and may actually have some information that would help him. He turned around and unlocked the door so he could go inside with Monica and find out what was so important. She sat on the couch, so he made sure to sit in the chair across from her just to keep some distance.

"Look, I know when I tell you this you are going to think I'm a piece of shit but I'm going to tell you anyway because you need to know it. Nahvi, Kelvin, and I have been fucking for a few weeks now."

"The fuck outta here. Ain't that nigga your best friend's baby daddy?"

"Yes and I know that I'm wrong, but I was lonely, Nahvi. After how I done you and then how Jared done me. I just needed to feel like someone cared and I mistook his dick for caring about me, but my karma slapped me in the face. I know you'll be shocked to hear me say this, but I deserved everything I got. I should have done better by you because you were good to me, even when you were still behind the gates. I'm sorry, Nahvi and I hope that one day you can find it in your heart to forgive me. I'm also sorry for the shit I said when your new girlfriend came here that night. I can look in your eyes and see that you are in love, and I don't want to fight with you or her. I just want you to be happy and wish I could have been the one to bring you that happiness."

Nahvi couldn't believe that Monica actually felt bad for all that she had put him through. He didn't want to hold any bitter feelings for her because walking around with bitterness in his heart could kill him. He did the only thing he knew to do. "I forgive you, Monica because deep down I know you have a heart, and you did make me happy for a long time. I don't know what happened but somewhere along the way, you lost sight of what mattered. I had planned to marry you and everything but sometimes plans just don't work out the way we want them to."

"Thanks Nahvi, you're a good man and I know that you deserve the best. However, I have more to tell you and it's going to piss you off when I do."

Nahvi looked at Monica and could feel her nervous energy. He wondered what could be so bad to make her feel that way. He wanted to make her feel more comfortable, so he got up and sat beside her. "Go ahead, Moni, you know that you can talk to me."

"Please don't be mad at me Nahvi because what I'm about to tell you is not what you want to hear. I'm the one who drove the Suburban into your truck. I knew after Kelvin sent that officer to pick you up you'd call her to come get your vehicle.

He knew that I held some animosity toward her, so he asked me to pull it off. I'm sorry."

Nahvi stood from where he sat because the beast in him told him to put some hot metal into the bitch in front of him. The only thing that stopped him was the fact that he knew how men could brainwash women and he also knew that Monica was weak minded. He had spent enough time with her to know that she was naive and believed anything.

"So, why you here telling me this shit now? What happened to bring you to my front door and don't fucking lie to me?"

Monica chose her words carefully, "Well, I told Tonya that me and Kelvin had been fucking around and she was pissed so she kicked me out. I didn't have anywhere to go so I went to Kelvin's house. A house that he didn't think I knew about. When I got there, some woman named Brandy answered his door. The bitch even acted like my presence didn't affect her. Kelvin finally came downstairs and made me feel like shit. He made me leave and told me he'd call me when he wanted to see me again. Nahvi, I felt so humiliated, and I couldn't believe that I had fallen for that bullshit. I lost you, my best friend and even myself but I want to make things right and I'm willing to do anything."

He thought about what she'd told him and decided that what she knew may be of some value to him. He had never known where Kelvin laid his head but now that he had access to that information, he would use it to his advantage.

"So, you say you know where that nigga lays his head at."

"Yeah Nahvi, I do."

"Come one and take a ride with me. I got a plan."

Corey Robinson

Chapter Twenty

When Nahvi pulled into the cut where Meek was at, Monica got nervous. "Um, why are you bringing me here?"

He looked over at her and answered. "You gonna tell my boy exactly what you told me."

Monica didn't want to tell Meek shit. She knew that he couldn't stand her ass, but little did he know, the feelings were mutual. She had already spilled the truth to Nahvi, and she didn't want to seem like she wasn't sincere, so she told Meek everything she had told Nahvi earlier. Nahvi made sure to watch her and listen to every word to make sure there was no flaw in her story, and he was impressed when none of her words got mixed up so that meant to him that she was telling the truth.

Meek couldn't believe his ears, but he knew too that Monica was telling the truth. Maybe she did feel bad for all the shit she had put Nahvi through and wanted to make things right.

"So, who all stay in that house you went to?"

"Well from what I could tell, it was only him and a bitch named Brandy. I'm pretty sure that not many people know about the house because he seemed surprised that I even knew where it was."

"And how exactly did you find out where it was?"

Monica did not want to answer Meek's questions because she was ashamed of it, but she had already came that far and wasn't no sense in backing out now. "I fucked his boy Talley, and he told me."

"Well damn, you just an old merry go round, ain't you?" Meek stated with a laugh and then turned to Nahvi. "Man I know you ain't know she was a hot like that but you may want to see how many other niggas she done been under. Lil momma gets around. How you know she telling us the truth, Nahvi? I mean the bitch did try to kill Ash so why should we trust her?"

Before Nahvi had a chance to answer, Monica cut in, "My story hasn't changed at all and I'm willing to show you where Kelvin lives. I'm tired of living like this and I just want to make amends."

Meek's nose flared because he would never be cool with Monica even if she did do the right thing. "How 'bout you make amends with God because if this don't pan out like it's supposed to, that's who I'm going to send your ass to. Do you fucking understand me?"

"Yes, Meek, I do, and I promise you I'm not up to no bullshit. I'm just trying to make things right."

Nahvi could read Meek's mind, so he knew what he was thinking without him ever saying it. He looked at Monica and said, "Go ahead and get back in the truck. I'm a take you back to the condo and let you chill there for a few days until we get this shit squared away. You cool with that?"

"Yeah Nahvi, I am, and you know I don't have anywhere else to go. I'd like to come out of this with at least a little of your respect."

Nahvi nodded towards the truck and Monica turned around and jumped back in. When he knew she wouldn't be able to hear, he said to his partner, "I'm a take this bitch back to the condo and drop her off. You get a hold of Packer and let him know what needs to be done. I'll meet you at the spot in one hour. Make sure you're ready when I get there."

Meek understood each and every word that Nahvi had said. He'd give Nahvi time to drop Monica off and leave and then he'd send Packer in. Packer was a young killer that Meek had on his team, and he was ruthless as a mufucka. He'd never missed a target and Meek knew that he would get results.

Packer was a street nigga that had been raised by the gun. His uncle had started him out at eight years old. He'd make him practice pulling a gun out while it was empty because he wanted young Packer to get used to the weight. Six months later, he filled the gun with bullets and took him out back in the woods where he'd made a gunman's paradise. He made replicas of all kinds of targets and taught him how to hit one every time. By the time Packer was ten, he could shoot a target with his eyes closed and still, he never missed. Meek ran in to him when he first started in the game. Packer was a jack boy but Meek saw more in him than that so he hired him as his own personal assassin and every time Meek needed someone to bleed, Packer would always come through.

Meek already knew that Nahvi wanted him to put Packer on Monica. She may have thought she was getting a second chance, but a snake can never change its appearance. No matter what it does, it will always be a snake. If Monica done fucked Kelvin and now sentenced him to death, she would do the same to anyone else. There was no way they could let her continue to breathe because she had proven her disloyalty over and over and to them. A disloyal muthafucka wasn't worth a damn."

"I got you, Nahvi. Send me a signal when you're gone, and I'll get the rest taken care of."

Nahvi got in his truck with Monica as his passenger and drove back to the place they used to call home. He felt bad about what was going to happen to her, but she had brought it all on herself. He couldn't risk her coming back for Ashley a second time, so he had to make sure she was taken care of. Things were quiet between the two until Monica finally spoke up. "Nahvi, if Kelvin finds out that I sold him out, you are going to protect me aren't you?"

He knew that Monica was afraid that Kelvin would send someone to retaliate but little did she know, Kelvin was the least of her worries. "Ah, now you know I ain't gonna let that nigga get close to you. Just sit back and chill and I promise you gonna be alright."

"Thanks for looking out for me. I really do appreciate it although I know that I don't deserve it."

"Nah, you good and you deserve this."

Nahvi pulled up in the driveway and Monica got out but before she shut the door he stated, "Aye, I'm a go get some food and shit and then I'll be back around to check on you."

"Alright, I'm a take a shower and shit. Thanks again." She shut the door and walked up the few steps that led to the front entrance of the house. She made sure to lock the door behind her and then she sighed in relief. She had always felt so safe in the condo and at that moment, there was nowhere else she'd rather be. Monica stripped down and decided to take a long, much needed bath so she could relax her mind. She made sure to put extra bubbles in the water and then wrapped her micros in a towel. She slid into the tub with ease and laid her head back falling into a soft slumber.

Nahvi texted Meek to let him know that he had left the condo and then he turned up the CD that he had playing. "Staying Alive" by DJ Khaled, Drake and Lil Baby came through the speakers and he bobbed his head to Drake's words, *First time I met her she was being a tease/Four pockets full, now she down on her knees.* The song was telling the truth because bitches always wanted to tease a mufucka with the pussy when his pockets were low but let them fill up with bread and they would drop to their knees without even being asked.

He thought back to before his pockets was laced. He was only fourteen and started slinging small amounts of Crack on the corners late at night when all the other dope boys went in. It wasn't a lot of money, but it was enough to feed him and pay Miss Rose for a back room at night. She told him he could stay there as long as he needed. She lived alone and sold hot plates to the people in the hood. Everyone had mad respect for her, and she never shut her door on someone in need. She said that she hoped someone would do the same if her grandson needed help. It helped Nahvi save some money and kept him safe from the eyes of DCF. The young girls would always flirt with him and try to tease him with the pussy but they asses ain't never wanna give it up. They told him that once he got his paper up to find them then, so, when Nahvi stepped out at eighteen years old, fly as a mufucka, those same bitches practically stripped without him having to ask but Nahvi was above that, and he fed them the same line they had fed him. "Nah, I'm cool but come see me when you get your paper up," and then he'd walk away and leave them standing there looking stupid.

He really did think that Monica was going to be different, but he was glad that he'd seen past her motives before it was too late. He pulled into the spot that him and Meek often met at and went inside so they could plan their moves.

Corey Robinson

Chapter Twenty One

Monica had earphones in her ears so there was no way she could have heard Packer come into the condo and make his way in the bathroom where she still laid back in the bubbles. Her mind was in all kinds of places, and she was trying to make sense of what she'd done with her life. When her cousin had called and informed her of Nahvi's status it made her pussy wet. She had been with so many different niggas and none of them had been worth a shit. They all treated her like shit. One day, she had finally met the man she thought would change her life and she was right. He changed it for the worse. So, when she seen the opportunity with Nahvi, she jumped on it. She had grown to care about him but deep down inside, her spirit and her heart had been too shattered to love anyone, including herself. Nahvi was a good nigga and his dick game could put any bitch in they place but she couldn't lie to herself. She had only rolled with him because his pockets were deep. She was honestly happy that he'd finally found someone he could really give his all to.

The water had started to become cold, so Monica decided to get out. She wanted to make sure she was dressed before Nahvi came back so he didn't think she was up to come shady shit. She pulled the ear plugs out of her ears and opened her eyes and thought that she had entered a nightmare. She didn't even have a chance to get the scream out before her head was pushed under water. The man held her there for a few seconds and then pulled her back up. He put a finger to his lips and told her to be quiet. "You be quiet, you stay safe." Those were his exact words but somewhere deep inside, Monica knew he was lying. She also knew that even if she screamed no one would hear her so she decided to play along hoping she'd eventually be able to get away. The towel was pulled from her micros and then the man grabbed a handful of them so he could drag her out of the bathtub. She didn't have her phone because she'd accidentally left it in Nahvi's truck. She hoped that he would notice and hurry back to return it to her, but Nahvi wasn't coming back anytime soon.

"Who are you and what do you want? Did Kelvin send you?"

"Ah come on now, do I look like a nigga who would ride with a mufucka like Kelvin? Don't insult my ego and don't worry about Kelvin, he's not going to come for you."

Monica thought that maybe the man had been there to protect her, and it relieved her mind a little. He had let her hair go and made her sit on the end of the bed. She was intrigued by his accent and wondered where he was from.

"Where I'm from doesn't matter. You should be more worried about where you are going."

He looked her naked body up and down and then licked his lips. He figured that it would be a waste to kill such a fine woman and not get him some pussy. "Lay back and let me look at you play with your pussy."

Monica cringed at the thought. "Hell no. Aren't you supposed to be protecting me instead of trying to fuck me?"

"Protect you? Now that's funny. You will do what I say, or you pay consequence. Your choice." Packer pulled out the gun from his waistband and put the cold tip on one of her nipples. "Now, do what the fuck I told you to do or you going to be sucking on this tip next."

Monica had never been raped in her life because she was used to giving the pussy away. She didn't know how to respond by someone forcing her to do things she didn't want to do. She slowly slid back on the bed and spread her legs. She willed herself not to cry because he may have been one of them men who got off from watching a woman shed tears out of fear. She put her fingers down on her pussy and did as he'd asked. Packer got hard quicker than he'd ever had so he pulled out his ten inches and mounted her. Monica knew that there was no use in fighting him, so she just lied there and took all of him. He didn't even have the decency to put on a condom, so she prayed that he didn't have any diseases and that she didn't get pregnant. She had the depo shot but she had heard stories of women still get pregnant while they were on them. He continued to pump into her until he came and then he pulled out and put a bullet in her head.

Packer pulled his clothes up and called the cleanup crew and then he walked out and left Monica to the angels.

He had left his ride on the block over from the condo, so he walked through the path that led to it making sure he was not seen. Only when he drove away was when he picked up the disposable phone and called Meek who answered on the first ring, "What's good, Pack?"

"Meek, what's going on? I'm just letting you know that I ain't going to be able to hang tonight so I'll have to catch you another time. Peace out, my man."

Meek knew exactly what the phrase meant so he turned to Nahvi and said, "Monica's done. You ready for the next?"

"Let's do it dawg. A nigga been ready for this shit."

The two men rode to the location that Monica had given them the address to. They were impressed that Kelvin had did so well for himself. The lights were still on in the massive estate, so they decided to sit it out. They could have put Packer on Kelvin too, but this shit was personal, so Nahvi wanted to handle it himself.

Meek sparked up a joint and leaned back in the seat so he could enjoy his high. When he tried to pass it to Nahvi, he refused. He wanted his mind to be clear for what was about to take place. He couldn't wait to put the nigga out of his misery and wanted to look him in the eyes when he did. The lights in the house begin to slowly go out so Meek and Nahvi prepared themselves. When the only light left on was one upstairs which the two men presumed to be the bedroom, they got out and pulled the facemasks over their faces. They decided to wear them until they were face to face with their victims just in case there was someone outside lurking. They couldn't afford to be identified.

Meek had already gotten a lay out of the house from one of the realtor chicks that he use to fuck with. He promised her some dick for the info, but Meek knew that he was just using that as ammo. He was really in to Tracey, and he didn't want to be known as a dog ass nigga. He usually stayed out of relationships so that way, he could do as he pleased but after fooling with Tracey, he decided to put a title on what they shared.

The two men made their way to the back patio by the pool. Meek pulled out a glass cutter and cut a square big enough for him and Nahvi to slide through the glass doors. He felt like it was the quietest way to enter. He had already known that there wasn't any alarms or cameras which was a dumbass mistake on Kelvin's part. Everybody knew that when you were deep in the drug game, you made sure the home was protected. That mistake would cost Kelvin dearly.

When the men were inside, they began to creep through the kitchen, but a sudden footstep stopped them in their tracks. They both stood with their backs against a wall and waited until the form came into view. When Nahvi saw that it was a female, he crept up behind her while she was in the refrigerator and put a hand over her mouth. They had only come there to kill Kelvin but if the bitch notified him of their presence, she could get her wig split too. Meek stood in front of her while Nahvi held her from behind and told her to be quiet. He pulled out a handkerchief and stuffed it in her mouth and then covered it with a piece of tape. Nahvi didn't know but Meek had already planned her demise too. He was always taught to never leave a witness behind because even though they couldn't see your face, you never could tell what else they had seen. For now though, they would tie her up and lock her in the closet.

They slowly crept upstairs and when they reached the top step, they heard Kelvin's voice, "Baby, go on down to the kitchen and see what's taking Brandy's ass so long. A nigga thirsty as fuck."

The naked Latino dropped Kelvin's dick from her mouth and did as he said. Kelvin's women knew not to defy him unless they wanted to be cut off. Brandy had been his main bitch for years and she knew about all of his rendezvous. She didn't give a fuck what he done in the streets or who he done it with as long as the dick laid beside her at night. Sometimes, Kelvin would bring women home so him and Brandy could enjoy them together. He loved the fact that she was so laid back and allowed him to be a man without any restrictions. That was why he'd never let her go.

The pretty Latino walked out of the room with nothing on to go on a mission to find her female lover, but before she made it to the bottom step she had a hand over her mouth and there was no way she could scream even if she wanted to. Nahvi held her while Meek tied her up too, and then they took her in a bathroom and laid her down in the tub. They hoped that there were no more surprises because they had already been in the house too long. They made their way back up the stairs and peeked in the room only to see Kelvin on the phone and smoking a blunt. They knew they would have to wait until he hung up before they could make a move so that way he couldn't alert anyone to their presence.

"Aye man, let me go down here and see what these bitches are doing. Mufuckas might be down there bumping without a nigga. Know what I'm saying?"

Kelvin laughed at his own comment and hung up. He placed the blunt in the ashtray and stood up but before he came out of the room he walked in the bathroom to take a piss. When he was done, he washed his hands and when he looked up that's when he saw the form behind him. "The fuck."

Before he could turn around, he heard the gun cock. "Don't even think about turning around too fast playa cause you gon' fuck up and get your shit split in half. Turn your ass around slow and walk back out the way you came. Kelvin had no choice but to do as the masked man said. The voice sounded familiar to him, but he was so nervous, he couldn't place it.

"Aye playa, why don't you just go ahead and open the safe and take what you want? This shit ain't over got to come to no bloodshed. We can work this out like two grown men." He didn't see the other masked figure until he came out of the bathroom. Kelvin knew then that the women downstairs were not coming back. "17-21-12."

"The fuck you telling me that shit for? That ain't why I'm here," The man said right before he pulled his mask off and revealed his face.

"Nahvi, man come on. Now you know I was just fucking with your ass for punching me in the mouth. A nigga wasn't gonna let you stay in there too long."

Meek pulled his mask off after Nahvi and then pushed Kelvin down on the bed. He held his gun steady and let Nahvi speak his peace while he held a gun on him too. "Nigga, this ain't about no damn arrest bullshit. This is about my mufuckin' girl and how you sent Monica's ass out with the Suburban."

Kelvin shook his head because he should have known that as soon as he dissed her in front of Brandy, she would be out for revenge. "So, I see her mouth is just as loose as that pussy. I knew I shoulda had that bitch taken out."

"Nah dawg, you ain't got to worry about that bitch or any other bitch. You should have kept that shit between us and kept my girl out of it. You wrong as fuck for that now you got to pay for that shit."

"I hope you lived a good life bitch cause that shit is over for you," Meek said right before Nahvi put one in Kelvin's dome.

The two men then went downstairs. Nahvi put his mask back on and started to walk out but when he saw that Meek wasn't behind him he turned back. When he heard the first muffled shot and then the second, he knew what Meek had stayed back to do. Meek came from the kitchen and met up with Nahvi and said, "Never leave witnesses behind even when you feel like you covered."

They walked back to the rental that they'd had parked and got in before they took off the masks. Meek picked up his phone and called the cleanup crew before he drove away. When they got back to the meet up spot, Nahvi jumped in his Denali and rushed to Ashley.

Corey Robinson

Chapter Twenty Two

"I'm really starting to worry, Tracey. He should have been back by now. He said he was just going to the condo to get some clothes and he'd be back, but it's been hours and now it's dark outside." Ashley had never worried over someone so much in her life, but she had reason to be because it seemed like so much bad shit followed Nahvi everywhere he went. She just didn't understand it.

"Girl, he'll be back. Him and Meek is probably somewhere together making that bread. We'll hear from them soon."

Ashley had seen a difference in Tracey ever since she'd been fucking with Meek. She seemed to have a glow about her, and she was much happier than she'd ever been with David. Ashley didn't want to pry but fuck it, she didn't have anything else to do. "So girl, how's things with Meek? You seem to be a whole different person now. That dick must be good to you."

Tracey raised her eyebrows and smiled at Ashley, and then answered her questions. "Oh Ashley, you were so right about going black. I mean, David is the only man I have to compare him to, but I am so gone. Girl, Meek is so good to me, and he spoils the hell out of me, and let a bitch try and disrespect me. His ass ain't having it. I got lucky with him, and you want to know a secret?"

Ashley sat up in her seat although her ribs still hurt a little, but she wanted to hear the secret Tracey held. "Bitch, you better spill it."

"We haven't been using protection and I think I'm pregnant."

"No. Oh my God. I'm going to be an auntie. What does Meek think about being a father?"

Tracey got quiet and that told Ashley all she needed to know. "Tracey, why haven't you told him yet? Don't you think that's something he needs to know?"

"I'm gonna tell him, Ash. I would never keep something like this from him, but I just found out earlier this morning. I wanted to wait until tonight after I make him some lasagna because that is what he loves. Then, we can relax and watch a movie or something and after he gives it to me real good, I'm going to tell him."

"You know you are good and silly but I'm so happy for you. I really am."

"Yeah, and when are you and Nahvi going to reproduce?"

Ashley thought about her question. She knew that she'd want children one day and now that she had the perfect man, she was more ready than ever. "Don't think I don't want a baby because I do, and I want it so much more with Nahvi, but we can't seem to get past all the damn drama in our lives. Plus, we've only had sex once."

Tracey shook her head because she couldn't believe that her friend was being greedy with the pussy. With a man like Nahvi, she should be giving it up every day. "I just really need to know how you can keep your legs closed with a man like that. Girl, that man is so damn fine. You better start spreading them bitches and let that man get in there."

"Yeah, I know and after my ribs heal, I'm gonna give it to him like a lady boss."

"Shit, ribs hurting or not, you better embrace that dick."

Nahvi walked in and heard them laughing and asked, "What's so funny in here?"

Ashley jumped up and winced in pain but ran into his arms anyway. "Where the hell have you been at, Nahvi? You can't keep making me worry like that. I'm gonna end up with wrinkles before I'm forty."

He pulled her close to him and kissed her forehead. He loved her so much and couldn't understand how he fell for her so quickly.

"Okay lovebirds, I'm leaving and going to my man now. I'll catch up with y'all later."

Tracey said her goodbyes and walked out so she could go let Meek know that he was going to be a father. When she left and they were all alone, all Ashley wanted to do was be held by him. They sat on the couch and talked and ended up falling asleep. The next morning, the sounds of the news reporter woke Ashley up and when she noticed that Nahvi was no longer next to her, she panicked but the voice pulled her into the latest update.

"Early this morning the police were called to the scene of a crime and recovered the body of known drug lord Kelvin Brown. He was found face down with a bullet hole in the back of his head. The police are blaming it on a drug war in the streets and so far there are no suspects in the case. We will keep you updated as the story develops. Thank you, back to you Tom."

Ashley couldn't find the words because the death of Kelvin had left her without any. No sooner than the story went off, Nahvi walked in the living room with a plate of food. Ashley looked at him and told herself that he couldn't have done it, but she still had to ask him so she could be sure.

"Nahvi, please tell me that you didn't have anything to do with Kelvin being shot."

His look alone answered the question that deep down she really didn't want answered. She never wanted to think of him as a cold blooded killer, but he was from the streets, and he did what he had to do to protect his family. She had become his family and she knew that she couldn't be mad for him wanting to rid her life of all that could harm her. She pulled him close to her and forgot about what she'd heard on the news. Nothing mattered more than what they shared, and she could only hope that he covered his tracks so that nothing could be led back to him.

Chapter Twenty Three

Nahvi spent a whole week inside with Ashley never once going to the streets but now it was time for him to make some moves. Meek had been blowing his phone up, but Nahvi told him every time he answered that he was spending some time with his woman. He had gotten the message from Meek telling him that Tracey was going to make him a father. Nahvi was happy for his friend and was more determined than ever to plant some seeds of his own. He had set up a meeting with Ashley and his realtor so she could go look at a house that sounded perfect for them. His realtor had also closed on the condo, and he put all the money from the sale in Ashley's bank account.

Things were going good for them again and with Kelvin and Monica both gone, it made it even easier, but Nahvi stayed alert because for some reason, his luck never lasted too long. He pulled up to the stash house to pick up some money and a crackhead from the block saw him and put a bug in his ear.

"Hey Nahvi, you throw me a little something and I'll tell you what I heard."

"Man get outta here with that shit."

"You may want to reconsider because it's been said that you had something to do with Kelvin Brown's murder."

When he heard that, he quickly turned his attention to the crackhead. He pulled a hundred dollar bill out of his pocket and passed it to the fiend.

"They say that Kelvin had two women up in the house with him and they both got shot but only one of them died. They say it's your name she's whispering from all of them tubes she hooked on. You may want to go check that out for yourself but my source is usually pretty good."

Nahvi couldn't understand how Kelvin was still haunting him from the grave. He couldn't believe that Meek hadn't made sure the women were both dead after he shot them. He had never known his friend to be so careless. He also wondered how she could have identified him because neither one of them had saw his face. He left the stash house quickly and called Meek. "Aye nigga, we need to meet up right now. Some shit being said, and we need to go find the source."

"Hello Nahvi, we've been waiting for your call. Meek's a little held up right now but you're more than welcome to join us. We'll be at the stash spot waiting for you. You do know the one I'm talking about right? It's the one you planned ol' boys murder in."

The phone went dead before Nahvi had a chance to respond. How the hell did Meek get caught sleeping like that? He wondered how word got out about the shit that went down.

Only him, Meek and Packer knew about them meeting and planning the murder of Kelvin. He knew for a fact that Meek didn't sell them out so that left one person. Meek said that Packer was solid but maybe he didn't know him as well as he thought or either Meek hit a target that meant something to him. Nahvi made sure his gun was loaded before he went to the spot to save his right hand. When he got there, just as he had assumed, Packer greeted him at the door. He walked inside and was stripped of his weapon after Packer searched him thoroughly.

Meek was taped to a chair and looked pretty rough. He could tell that he had been beaten really bad and wondered for how long. "I'm here now so tell me what's up."

Packer paced the floor and replied while holding a gun in his hand the entire time. "I took care of Monica for you while you were supposed to handle Kelvin, but you never said that any harm would come to Brandy."

"Man, you know how the shit goes and you knew we couldn't leave a witness behind. She had to go. What the fuck is it to you anyway? That was Kelvin's bitch."

"Yeah it was. But his bitch was also my sister. I never liked Kelvin's ass, but Brandy loved him and as long as she never came to me with a broken heart, I stayed out of it. I gave her my word that I'd never feed him a bullet but when the opportunity for someone else to do it presented itself, I couldn't pass it up."

"Then, you also knew how shit went. You can't fault us for that. You should have said something ahead of time, especially since you knew she would be there. Her death is on you so it's your own hands you should be washing."

Nahvi remembered the crackhead telling him about the woman laid up in the hospital still alive and asked. "What about the one still alive? What you know about her since we ain't had no warning about your sister? You gonna avenge her too?"

"Fuck her. She can lay where she's at and die too because I ain't worried about her telling shit. I don't care if she drops your name because ain't neither one of you walking up outta here."

Meek sat bound in the chair and thought about the baby that Tracey was carrying. He was finally going to be a father and yet, he would never meet his child. He hoped that Nahvi came up with a plan really quick to help them both out because he couldn't do anything. Hell, he could barely see out of his swollen eyes. He had never felt so defeated in his life or so helpless. He couldn't believe that he'd had Packer up under him for all those years and never knew that the bitch Kelvin Brown had wifed up was his sister. Packer was a private person, but Meek was sure he would have at least talked about family. The whole crew knew that family was off limits, but one has to know who that family was in order to protect them. Packer brought it on himself to have to mourn her so the gun he held on Nahvi should have been pointed the other way.

"Come on, Pack, you know that we didn't know she was family. We would have spared her if you would have told us. You can't fault us for this one. "Nahvi could see Packer's hand tighten on the trigger and thought about Ashley. He hated that he'd had such a short amount of time with her, but he knew that the streets showed no type of mercy. Out there, it was an eye for an eye, and he had to pay his dues.

Packer walked up closer to him but kept enough distance between them to keep Nahvi from fighting for the gun. He wanted Meek to watch someone he cared about suffer the same fate as Brandy and since he didn't know that Meek had a pregnant girlfriend at home, his best friend became the target. "I hope you've said your final goodbyes."

Nahvi closed his eyes and sent a quick prayer to his creator for Ashley. She was all he had left that meant anything to him. He waited for the bullet to strike him and when he heard one gun go off, he flinched but never fell. He actually didn't even feel an ounce of pain, so he opened his eyes to see what had happened. He wondered if Packer changed his mind and shot Meek instead. How was he going to tell Tracey that her baby would grow up without a father? He knew how that shit felt to be without one because his ran off before he even came out of the womb and the one that his mother used as a substitute had taken her from him.

Nahvi couldn't believe what he was looking at when his eyes opened completely. Packer was on the ground in a pool of blood while Ashely stood over him with a gun in her hand. How did she even know where to find him? "Ash, what the hell are you doing here?"

She ran up to him and he embraced her. He felt his tears and wondered how she could make a grown man feel so much joy that his eyes watered. "I followed you, Nahvi and I know you're probably angry about that but here lately, every time you leave the house something bad happens and I just couldn't sit there and worry anymore. I had to come rescue you. I couldn't imagine living without you."

Nahvi kissed her deeply and then remembered Meek, "Come on baby, we gotta get Meek some help."

They rushed to his side and untaped him and he was so weak he almost fell out of the chair. They picked him up and carried him to Nahvi's truck so they could get him to the hospital. When they got there, Nahvi thought about the woman that Meek had shot and knew that she was in there somewhere. He waited until the nurses got Meek settled and turned to Ashley. "Hey, you stay here and wait for my boy, I gotta go check something out."

Ashley smiled at him and whispered in his ear, "Don't worry baby, I've already taken care of her too."

He couldn't believe his ears but was overcome with joy. He would wait until they got home to question her because he didn't know who could hear him. They sat together and appreciated the time they had. Ashley opted not to call Tracey because she didn't want to put stress on her and the baby. She knew that Meek had only suffered a few cuts and bruises. He was a soldier and he would pull through. They sat and waited for almost an hour until Meek finally emerged. "Nigga, I don't know what you sitting around pouting like a bitch for. You know a mufucka can't do nothing with me."

Nahvi jumped up as soon as he heard his voice and gave his friend a hug. His eyes were still swollen but at least they were open. He looked like shit, but he was alive and that was all that mattered to all of them. "Ah man, I'm sorry. I couldn't do shit when I got there but that nigga had me against the wall."

"I know man, it's all good. My sis in-law came through though. Where the hell did you learn to do all that?"

Ashley wrapped her arms around Nahvi and replied. "Boy, I know you don't think I've dated street thugs all my life and didn't learn anything. I got some skill. Plus, did you really think that I could let someone take this wonderful man away from me? I'd rather die than live without him."

When Nahvi dropped Meek off at home, Tracey burst into tears as soon as she saw him. Nahvi was so happy that his boy was still around. He had so much to be thankful for. Him and Ashley had seemed to pull through so much. When they got home, Nahvi didn't waste any time showing her how thankful he was. As soon as they walked in the door, he pulled her in for a kiss. His dick became hard instantly and he couldn't wait to have it inside of her. They had only managed to make love once and now he wanted to make up for it. He wouldn't hold anything back from her.

Nahvi pulled her shirt off and then her bra. He stood for a minute and admired her beauty. She was like a porcelain masterpiece. Ashley's voice broke him from the trance, "Well, are you just gonna stand there and look at it or are you gonna do something with it?"

Damn, she turned him on. He picked her up and carried her to the bedroom where he knew that he'd have plenty of room to give her what she needed. When he had stripped her completely, he took off his clothes and then spread her open. He wanted to taste her sweet vanilla essence, so he pulled her clit into his mouth and brought her to the edge of pleasure.

"Oh, Nahvi baby, yes. That feels so good. Oh baby, you're gonna make me cum."

He liked the sound of that because that was his intention. He sucked harder and slowly inserted a finger into her warmth. He felt her legs shake and when she erupted, he pulled his finger out and replaced it with his tongue. He could get full off of just her sweetness. After she came, he was about to push into her but Ashley had a different idea.

"Uh uh, lay down. This time is on me."

He did as his snow queen told him and couldn't wait to see what she had in store for him. She grabbed his manhood and slowly began to shake it. His thickness filled her hand to capacity, but she liked it. She reached her other hand down, massaged his nutsack and then pulled the head of his dick in between her lips. She savored the salty yet sweet flavor of his pre cum as she deep throated him. She slowly and carefully sucked him until he was almost to his peak. Ashley wanted his seeds inside her womb not her stomach, so she let him fall from her mouth and straddled him.

Nahvi grabbed her hips as she rode him.

"God, you feel so good inside of me, Nahvi. Oh baby, I could do this all day with you."

Nahvi couldn't have agreed more. Ashley was the best love he'd ever had, and he never wanted to be inside another woman because it wouldn't feel the same to him. When he came, he felt like the earth shook around him because of the intensity. He was sure he planted the seeds in the right place and hoped to have made some little ones from it. They made love several times after that and then finally fell asleep in each other's arms.

The next morning it would be business as usual. He would meet up with Meek while Ashely and Tracey worked with the movers to get their new home ready. Ashley had found them a cozy four bedroom, four and a half bath mini mansion with a huge backyard for their future children to play in. Tracey had went with her to view the house and noticed the one next door was up for sale too. She talked to Meek and he agreed that it would make sense for them to live side by side. So while their men were in the streets, the women were making houses into homes.

Chapter Twenty Four

When Meek and Nahvi hit the streets, no one said a word about what had happened to Kelvin and Monica. They expected someone to strike back and avenge Kelvin's death, but no one did. They were surprised but found out that his crew was happy about him being gone. He never treated any of them as equals and paid them just enough to keep their feet on the ground. Even his right hand said that Kelvin got just what he had deserved.

Nahvi thought about his upcoming retirement from the block and wondered if he could talk Meek in to retiring too but Meek wasn't so easily swayed. "Hey Meek, nigga you ain't never thought about getting out of this shit. Maybe sitting back and enjoying the fruits of your labor. Don't you think it's time, man? I mean you do have a child coming into this shit. Is that what you want for them?"

Meek thought about what Nahvi said and then answered. "Nahvi, I live for this shit. I couldn't even imagine a life without being out here in these streets. I mean, I know that they may very well one day be the death of me but until then, I gotta keep pushing. These same streets been good to a nigga so ain't no way I can turn my back on 'em."

"Aiight man, you know I got your back no matter what, but I think this last run we do is gonna be just that for me, a last run. I'm trying to think about my future with Ash and these streets ain't where it's at."

Nahvi convinced his own self that the words he'd spoken were true but two months later, he was still in the trenches and saw no end in sight. It seemed as if him and Meek dove even deeper ever since they had eliminated Kelvin. The streets solely belonged to them, and they took advantage of it for as long as they could, but as always, things didn't go as planned for very long. The way that the money was coming in there were bound to be haters lurking in the dark and that put everything they had worked so hard for at risk.

When Nahvi's phone rang and he saw who the caller was, he already knew there was about to be drama.

"Nahvi, this is Tonya and I need for you to stop by and see me. You got some shit to explain and you can give me the answers I'm looking for or you can give them to the police, bitch."

She hung up as soon as she got the words out of her mouth, and Nahvi already knew that she was going to question him about Kelvin and Monica so he looked to Meek and said, "Yo Meek, we might have a small problem bro. That was Tonya and she talkin' that shit. You think she knows something about what happened?"

"Nah nigga, ain't no way she could know. Mufuckas been stopped talking about it. Dumb bitch just probably trying to pick your ass. That's all. You want me to go with you over there?"

"Nah Meek, I can't handle Tonya's dumb ass . I'll holla at you when I leave there."

Nahvi got in his own ride and headed to Tonya's. He hoped that he wouldn't have to kill her too because he didn't want to leave Kelvin's son with no one. He pulled up into her complex and got out, but he wasn't ready for what he walked into.

Tonya had on just a T-shirt and smiled when she opened the door and looked at him, but he wasn't thrilled about the visit. "The fuck you talking about on that phone? You call yourself threatening me with some shit I don't know anything about?"

He walked all the way in and when Tonya shut the door behind him she pulled the T-shirt from over her head. "Well,

I'm sorry I had to make you feel threatened, but I felt like that was the only way I could get you to stop by."

Nahvi headed back to the door because he wasn't about to get caught up in Tonya's fantasy. He knew that she'd always had a thing for him when he was with Monica, but she'd never done no shit like she was doing then. Nahvi tried not to react but when his dick swelled Tonya noticed. She walked up to him, and he knew that he should have backed away but for some reason his feet wouldn't move.

"You should let a real bitch take care of that for you. Monica didn't know how to appreciate it." She unzipped his jeans and stuck her hand inside his boxers. When she pulled the beast out, he didn't stop her. He thought about Ashley as she stroked his massive dick. Nahvi knew that he would be dead wrong to let what was going on get any further but before he could say anything, Tonya already had him in her mouth. She was bent over and when he looked at her bare ass cheeks, he couldn't help but grab one. He gripped her ass so tight that he left marks.

"Shit. Damn, you feel good."

Tonya smiled to herself while sucking his dick at the same time. She deep throated that motherfucker and Nahvi watched as it disappeared down her throat. He couldn't just stand there and do nothing, so he slid a finger into her wetness. He could hear her moans from below and it made him thrust his finger deeper. He didn't mind cumming inside a bitches throat, but it always felt better when he was deep in some guts.

He pulled back from Tonya because he was ready for more. He continued to tell himself to turn around and walk out but still, he didn't listen. He knew that he had already gone too far so why back out. "Turn around and let me bust this nut. And remember, you asked for this shit."

Tonya turned around and when she did he pushed her into the wall and entered her from behind. Tonya felt like he was going to split her open, but she didn't want him to stop. "Oh God, yes Nahvi. Fuck me hard nigga. Give me every inch of you."

When he found himself about cum, he pulled out and stroked his dick. After a couple of strokes, he came all over Tonya's ass cheeks. He couldn't lie to himself; she had some good pussy and although he knew that he had did the ultimate betrayal, he felt like it was worth it, and he knew that Ashley would never find out. It was a one time thing and how was he supposed to stop his dick from reacting to Tonya's advances. He stood behind her and caught a second wind just in time for her to turn around and wrap her hand around him again. He had already violated the code and he knew that what he was doing would be unforgivable.

Tonya finished undoing his jeans and then slid them down his long tattooed legs. Because he had just fucked her with his pants still up, she knew the fresh smell of her sex would be on his jeans. She hoped that his grimey ass got found out by the white girl. She knew that it was because of Nahvi and Meek that Kelvin was gone. There was no way for her to prove it but deep in her gut, she knew, and she was just paying them back. She'd make sure to get up with Meek another day. She had Nahvi sit down on the couch and then she turned on a slow jam and danced dirty for him. He was amazed at how she made her fat ass jiggle, and it only made him hungry for another piece of her.

She turned her back to him, spread her ass and slid down onto him. The deep arch in her back was sexy to him and as she rode him, he ran a finger down the middle of it. She kneaded his nuts while she grinded on him and he could feel another nut coming about to be released. "I'm 'bout to cum again. Make that pussy cum with me. She put her finger on her clit as Nahvi pushed a thumb in her backside and together they burst with satisfaction. When he came, he forgot about being inside of her. So, he filled her with his seeds. Tonya on the other hand knew exactly what she'd just done.

She came off of him and said while she stood in front of him and breathed heavily. "Nigga, you know that this is a one time shot so I hope you enjoyed yourself. Don't ever come back here again." Nahvi was confused but he managed to pull up his pants and walk out. He decided it would be best to get the hell out of dodge. He couldn't believe that he had fallen weak like that and felt like maybe he should do the right thing and tell Ashley but that thought left as quickly as it had come. Little did he know, he wouldn't have to tell her because she was going to see picture as clear as day.

There was no way he could go home yet because his guilt was eating him up inside. He called Meek to meet him.

"You did what? Nah Nahvi, please tell me that you are just fucking with me."

"I wish I could man, but I can't. I'm not one of those dog ass niggas but something happened, and I fell weak, and I don't know what to do."

"Uh, you did wear protection, didn't you?"

The way Nahvi looked at Meek answered his question. He knew that what happened with Tonya was wrong but him not using protection would only make shit worse. "Damn man, I don't know what the hell I was thinking. The fuck am I going to do?"

"You gonna take your ass back over there and slip that bitch an abortion pill. That's what the fuck you going to do." About that time, Meek's phone vibrated. He thought it was Tracey, so he answered. "Sup baby, you missin' a nigga right now?"

When he found out it was Tonya, he hit Nahvi in the arm and held up a finger so he wouldn't speak.

"Nah Tonya, I thought you was my girl but what's up?"

When she asked him to stop by, he laughed at her suggestion. "The fuck do you think I am? Some kind of dumbass mufucka? Nah bitch, that ain't about to happen." He hung up on her and turned to Nahvi. "She just told me the same shit you said she told you. That bitch is on some get back but we going to get that ass first. I'll come get you tomorrow and we can ride over there together. I'll hold that bitch down and make her swallow that pill. You got to make sure that bitch don't have no kind of proof of what y'all done and a baby could damn sure expose it."

"Aiight man, damn." Nahvi pinched the bridge of his nose with worry. He knew that something like that could ruin what he had with Ashley, and he loved her with all his heart. He got out of Meek's ride and jumped in his own so he could return home. He just hoped that his sin didn't show on his face.

Chapter Twenty Five

When Ashley opened her eyes, the morning sun nearly blinded her. She reached over to touch the man she loved but his side of the bed was empty. He never left without saying something just in case it was the last time he saw her. She knew that something was wrong because everything Nahvi felt, she felt too. She hoped that when he came back home he would tell her what was on his mind.

Ashley got out of bed and went in the bathroom to get herself together. The warm water that flowed from the shower head relaxed her mind and body. She still ached sometimes from the trauma she'd suffered in the crash, but she refused to let anything get her down. No sooner than she got dressed she heard the doorbell ring. She thought maybe Tracey was feeling sick again and needed some comforting, so she sped to the door to answer it. When she opened it, she didn't see her best friend looking back at her but instead a delivery man.

"Hi. Can I help you with something?"

"Yes, I'm looking for an Ashley Taylor. I have a delivery for her, and I need her to sign for it."

"Oh, well that's me but I'm not expecting anything." She reached her hand out to accept the small envelope and signed the invoice. The man smiled at her, and she wasn't sure if he was flirting or just being friendly.

"Have a nice day, ma'am." He stated and Ashley shut the door so she could open the package. The brown envelope contained a VHS tape, something she hadn't seen in a while. She didn't even know they still made them because DVD players were the new thing. However, Nahvi had a VCR in the garage in one of his storage bins, so she went out to retrieve it. It took her a little digging around, but she finally located what she was looking for.

She decided to hook the VCR up to the small television in the kitchen. She wasn't the best when it came to electronics, but a child could hook one of the old machines up. She began to get excited because she thought that Nahvi had sent her a little surprise and she couldn't wait to view it. When she had it hooked up, she pulled the tape out of its case and noticed that the date written on it was the day before, but she also noticed that the handwriting was too neat to be her man's. The script looked too feminine for his hard exterior.

She shrugged and pushed the tape inside but when it started she was a little confused at first because she saw Nahvi and Kelvin's son's mother talking. When she saw Tonya remove her shirt, she looked closer. She saw Nahvi walk to the door as if he were going to leave but instead Tonya stopped him. Tears formed in Ashley's eyes at the sight of what she was watching. The video wasn't fixed. It was all real and he couldn't lie and say that it was old because the chain he wore around his neck was one she'd gifted him with only a few days earlier. She thought that she would be sick on her stomach but she couldn't will her eyes to leave the screen.

She heard Tracey calling her name, but she couldn't even respond. Ashley felt like her feet were stuck in concrete and her heart was buried in it. "Ash, girl what the hell are you doing? Didn't you hear me calling you?"

Tracey walked up behind her but when her eyes landed on the screen she stopped. "Oh my God, Ashley. Turn it off. You shouldn't be looking at that."

"No, I want to see it all the way through."

"Oh Ashley, I'm so sorry." Tracey reached over and turned the machine off and the images on the screen disappeared. She didn't know what to say so she said nothing at all. She pulled her friend in and held her as the tears soaked her maternity shirt. She couldn't believe that Nahvi could be so heartless and cold. Ashley had once again gave her all and now her heart was broken. Tracey was about to call Meek and tell him how foul his boy was, but Ashley stopped her. She would deal with it herself. Tracey could only respect what she asked of her, so the two women sat and waited for the culprit to show up, but little did they know the men they loved were across town handling some business of their own.

Corey Robinson

Chapter Twenty Six

Tonya opened the door and the two men rushed in. "What the hell are y'all doing?"

Meek grabbed her by the neck and pushed her against the wall. She could feel her breath leaving her slowly as she tried to pull Meek's hand away, but he was just too strong for her. Nahvi pulled the syringe out of his pocket and pulled in the abortion pills that they had crushed and made into a liquid. They wanted to make sure it worked just in case Nahvi's little fuck up had planted some seeds.

Meek picked up one of her arms and held it against the wall too. However, she never gave up her fight. When Nahvi grabbed her free arm, he quickly found a vein and injected the substance into her arm. Tonya didn't know what they had just shot inside of her, but the thought caused her to give up.

When Meek let her go, she slid down to the floor and started coughing but when she was able to catch her breath she asked. "What in the hell did you just inject in me? Please tell me it wasn't Heroin. I got a son to take care of."

Meek spoke up first, "Nah, it was just a little something to make sure that you don't have his little ass any siblings and try to put it on my boy here."

She looked to Nahvi while he stared back at her with death in his eyes. "I'm on the shot, you couldn't have gotten me pregnant. You didn't have to do what you just did. Besides, what you didn't know was that I recorded the whole thing. The tape should have arrived in your bitches hands less than thirty minutes ago, dated and all. So, you could have saved the bullshit you came here with."

Meek hauled off and slapped her. "You stupid bitch. You know when we came here we had no intentions of hurting you but now, bitch you 'bout to get your karma." He pulled out a gun and aimed it at her head, but Nahvi reached over and pulled the gun from his hand.

"Nah Meek, let me do it. I caused this bullshit so let me handle it." Nahvi pointed the tip of the gun at Tonya's head and just as he was about to pull the trigger a movement caught his eye. He turned his head toward that movement and saw a face that looked just like Kelvin.

"Ma Ma," The small boy cried out and began to walk toward Tonya but before he could make it to her Meek swooped him up.

"No, please not my son. I'm sorry Nahvi but you left me no choice. You took Kelvin from me and no matter how many times you deny it, I know it was you. You two hated each other. What happened? Did you find out he was fucking Monica? Did that set you off?

Nahvi slapped her to shut her up and when he did, Kelvin Junior started to cry. It reminded him of all those times he cried when he watched his own mother get hit.

"Meek, get the boy outta here."

Meek turned and walked into the kid's bedroom and shut the door behind him, but Nahvi could still hear him cry for his only provider. Nahvi had already taken his father. Could he really be so cold and take his mother too? He looked in her eyes and thought about what she'd done and how she had possibly ruined his future with Ashley.

"What are you going to do to my son? Please don't hurt him. You can't possibly be that cruel. Please Nahvi, I'm sorry for real."

Nahvi got up and left Tonya sitting there. He opened the door to the room that Meek went in with the kid and stated, "Leave the kid and let's go."

Meek nodded and rubbed the kid on the head before he walked out. When he saw that Tonya was still alive, he looked at Nahvi confused but didn't ask him any questions. He decided to wait until they were in the ride. He gave Tonya one final glance and walked out in front of Nahvi. When they made it to the ride and got in, Meek wanted to know what happened. "Nigga, what the fuck happened back there? Why is that bitch still breathing?"

"I couldn't kill her, Meek. When that little boy came out and saw me put my hands on her it made me think of my momma. I watched her get beat on all my life so I knew how that kid felt. The least I could do was leave him somebody behind who loves him because I was left with nobody and dawg, that shit hurts.

"What about the shit she pulled? And she said she sent a recording to ya girl. How you thinking that shits going to work out for you?"

Nahvi shrugged and replied, "What happened between us was partly my fault. I should have been stronger, but I wasn't. I could have stopped her at any time, but I didn't, so to kill her for that foul shit wouldn't be right. I got to man up and take some of that blame."

Meek understood what Nahvi was saying and if Tonya really had sent a tape of what happened to Ashley, then killing her would all be for nothing. The damage had already been done. "So, what you gon' do if Ash leaves your ass?"

"Then, I'm gonna tuck in my tail and walk away."

Corey Robinson

Chapter Twenty Seven

When Nahvi walked in the house, he expected to be cursed the fuck out but instead the house was quiet. He prayed that Ashley hadn't already left him without giving him a chance to explain. Although, he knew he didn't deserve one. He tried to imagine a life without her but there wasn't one. Hell, there wasn't even one before her so how would he go on. There was no excuse for what he'd done. He was only being a man, a weak one who loved his woman but couldn't stand strong to honor her. His mother would have been so disappointed. She'd always told him that a man who cheats ain't really a man.

He finally walked upstairs to their plush bedroom. He looked around and admired its beauty. He had done well for himself and now it no longer excited him to have it. When he saw Ashley's form lying in their bed, his heart skipped a beat. He could already feel her heartbreak from a far but now that he was closer, it felt like a full heart attack.

"Are you just going to stand there and stare at me or are you going to come to bed?"

The sound of her voice broke him from his thoughts. It made him wonder if Tonya had really done what she said because if she hadn't then maybe he was in the clear. He kicked off his shoes and undressed but before he got in the bed, he took a quick rinse off. He always liked to wash away his streets deeds before he went to bed at night. While he was in the shower, he told himself that he would clear his conscience. There was no way he could lie beside the woman he loved with such a heavy burden in his heart.

He opted to sit on the edge of the bed beside her just in case she wanted him away from her once he said what he had to say. "Ash, I need to talk to you and it can't wait. There's something I need to tell you."

"It's okay, Nahvi, I already know. She sent it to me, and I've watched it over and over so there's nothing left for you to say."

"Baby, I'm sorry. I never wanted to hurt you in any kind of way." Nahvi got up to walk out of the room because he felt unworthy of her presence, but Ashley spoke up. "You don't have to leave, Nahvi. You're a man and sometimes you get weak. I understand that. You were dead ass wrong and at any given moment, you could have walked away but your mind overstepped its boundaries. I'm not excusing what you done and it's something I won't put up with but I'm going to let you have that one slip up but anything after that, I won't forgive you for."

Nahvi couldn't believe his ears. What kind of woman forgave a man for his infidelities? "So, you're saying that you forgive me?"

"Yes Nahvi, I forgive you. I forgave Kelvin for so much more so why can't I do the same for you? I love you and I know that you love me too, but you have hurt me to my inner core. Now, come here baby because you have some serious making up to do."

She threw the covers off of her naked body and pulled Nahvi into her embrace. She kissed him with a passion hot enough to start a fire. Her erect nipples would surely cut sharp as a knife. Ashley straddled him and held him so tightly he felt like he would stop breathing. He knew in his heart that he would never hurt her that deeply again. He wondered how such a wonderful woman had come into his life and changed everything. He would cherish her always. He stood with her still in his arms and then turned around to lay her down. He had only opened up pieces of himself to her but that night, he would open up completely and give his all. Everything he held inside of him he would share it and put it in her hands because he knew that with her, he was safe from anything that had held him back. They made love the rest of the night and then lie there and just held each other.

Ashley told him about the family that had disowned her at a young age. She was only fourteen when she realized that she'd had an attraction to black guys. Her mother told her to follow wherever her heart led her, but her father told her that no daughter of his would be bringing black children into the world and he banned her from even talking to them. Ashley got along better with the black kids, so she continued to hang out with them. The white kids were too uppity for her with the exception of Tracey who never judged her.

When her father came to the school unexpectedly and saw her holding hands with a black boy, he sent her across town to live with her grandmother, but little did he know, she would allow Ashley to live her life to the fullest. She always told her, "You can't help what you like and as long as it makes you happy, nothing else matters."

Tracey's parents would let her come spend the weekends with her so they could share all of their gossip and when Ashley tried to make amends with her father, he didn't want to hear it and disowned her from that day on. She didn't know where her parents were now and honestly didn't care. She was happy and the last thing she needed was for her father to ruin all she had obtained.

Nahvi told her about his mother and how she died at the hands of the man she loved. His life hadn't been so great after that, but he had managed to make the best of it. He still held a deep hatred deep in his soul for the man who took her from him and hoped that he never saw him again because he still wanted to kill him.

"Nahvi, I know this may sound crazy, but you have to forgive him and let go of that bitterness because it will eat you up inside."

"Forgive him? The fuck is wrong with you? How the hell am I supposed to do that?"

"You can. You may not realize it but if you go deep inside of your heart, you'll find the strength. Do it for your mother, Nahvi. He was wrong for taking her life but honey. He has paid his debt and I'm sure he feels bad but even if he doesn't, don't let him have that control over you because as long as you still hold that feeling for him, he has the reigns."

Nahvi heard what she was saying but it still made no sense to him. What Ashley didn't know was that the man would be getting released soon and when he did, Nahvi planned on being there.

Chapter Twenty Eight

"So, you saying that she forgave you just like that? No questions asked."

"Yeah, Meek, she did it just like that."

Meek was happy that the incident with Tonya didn't tear Nahvi and Ashley apart. Him and Tracey had ended up being perfect for each other and he wondered if he ever cheated on her, would she be as forgiving. He didn't even have time to dwell on his answer before he saw the flashing lights behind him. "Oh shit, yo man. We got some company."

"Shit. I hope you kissed your girl goodbye," Nahvi said and held his head down because they were dirty and had no time to clean up. They had always been careful but that night they seemed relaxed and should have known it only meant disaster especially when the cop that had pulled them over was one of Kelvin's. They was sure he was feeling salty since Kelvin was no longer around to pay his bills.

Meek rolled his window down as soon as the officer got up on them. He didn't know that he'd already called for backup, but he would soon find out. "What seems to be the problem officer?"

"Step out of your vehicle very slowly and walk to the front of it with your hands up."

Both men had guns on them that they planned to throw on the side of the road as soon as they made it to the front. The drugs were stashed in a hidden compartment. They could only hope that they were not found because since the cop used to work for a known drug dealer, he had to know about the hidden spots. No sooner than they pulled out their guns and threw them, another police car pulled up with two officers inside.

One of them whispered something to the other one and he walked to where the men had threw the guns at. Nahvi and Meek were completely blindsided when the cop that had stopped them popped open the floorboard and found the compartment that held two bricks of pure cocaine.

As soon as Meek and Nahvi were transported to the station, one of them called the lawyer while the other called home. They both knew that shit like that happened in their line of work but they both manned up and said nothing. Of course you always had the one cop who tried to play them against each other, but Meek and Nahvi were thoroughbreds.

"Mr. Johnson, as you know, my boys found two kilos of pure cocaine in the floorboard of the vehicle you happened to be driving. On top of that, the officers that pulled up to assist observed both of you throw something and upon further inspection, they found it to be guns. So, unless only one of you held two guns that is going to be five years. However, your boy is a convicted felon, so you already know it's not going to work out for him. So tell me, was it his cocaine too? You might as well save yourself."

Meek stared a hole through the officer but said nothing. He wouldn't without his lawyer present. He'd lay down and do life before he turned snitch on anyone, even if it were his enemy. He had never been in trouble before and if he had to, he'd take the gun charges too just to keep his boy from getting a lot of time. Meek was solid like that.

Across the hallway in another room, Nahvi was questioned by another investigator. "Mr. Karter, we fingerprinted both guns and one of them came back with your prints on it. From what I see here, you were recently released after doing eight years, which makes you a convicted felon. That's not good for you so I'm willing to help you out but I'm gonna need something from you in return. What do you say?"

Nahvi continued to stare the officer in the eyes but kept his mouth closed. He didn't give a fuck what the crooked investigator offered; he had nothing to tell them. The man in front of him slammed his hand on the desk and stood. He bent down until he was face to face with Nahvi and continued his rant. "You know your boy Ahmeek Johnson told my partner that those two kilos belonged to you, and he didn't even know they were in the vehicle. You may never see the light of day again if he testifies against you, so you better think real hard about what you're going to do. I'm sure that pretty little lady that showed up to check on you ain't gonna wait all those years for some dick."

Nahvi stood and drew back his fist but stopped before he made contact. He knew that he was giving the man just what he wanted, and he didn't want to do that. He sat back down and thought about what the man had said. He knew that he was lying because he knew Meek would give his life for him and he would do the same. Nahvi wasn't a dumb nigga and all the cracker in front of him would get was pure silence.

"Okay, Mr. Karter. That's how you want to play things. I'm not the one facing prison time, you are, and I'm going to do all I can to push it." The investigator finally walked out and left Nahvi alone but a few minutes later, the door opened again, and his lawyer walked in.

"Sorry it took me so long to get here but I was at an important meeting trying to prepare for another case. I haven't been able to talk to Mr. Johnson yet, but I'll see him as soon as we're done." The lawyer opened his briefcase and pulled out a file and then proceeded. "Looks like they found the two kilos unlawfully because I'm not seeing anywhere when a search warrant was used."

"That's because they didn't have one. We were stopped and then made to get out of the vehicle, and he searched while the other two officers held us."

"Did he even ask for permission to search?"

"Nah, his ass just made us get out and stand in front of the car. Apparently, he'd already called back up because those officers came not even two minutes after he pulled us over."

"Okay, so I can get those charges thrown out for an illegal search and seizure. However, we have a problem with this gun charge. Your fingerprints were found on one of the guns that the officer's found in the grass beside where you were stopped. Mr. Karter, I'm not so sure that I could make this charge disappear, but I can argue to get you very little time."

"Time, man come on. I just made up with my girl. I can't afford to go back to prison now. There's got to be something you can do." Nahvi held his head in his hands and then ran them over his face out of frustration. How could he have been so stupid? The news would break Ashley's heart and he had promised her that he'd never break it again. How would he be able to live without her for that long? He wondered if she'd ride the time with him or walk away. He knew she loved him, but he wondered if love was enough. "How much time are we talking about?"

The lawyer pursed his lips together and looked down at the papers laid out on the table in front of him and then looked up at Nahvi. "Well, just having possession of the weapon is five years but with you being a convicted felon that has been out less than three years, I could work out maybe a ten year deal."

"Nah, me and Meek pay you too much to get me ten. I'll plea out for three."

The lawyer looked at Nahvi like he was crazy, but he knew that he was serious. He gathered up his paperwork and put it back in his briefcase before he stood. He looked at Nahvi one last time. "I'll see what I can do, Mr. Karter. Have a nice day." And then he walked out.

He walked across the hall to see Meek and told him about the conversation he had with Nahvi. Meek didn't want his boy to go back to the pen, but he knew it was going to happen and there wasn't shit he could do to stop it. No matter how much time he got, he would stick by him and make sure his girl had all she needed, and when he got out, he'd have him then too. Meek knew that since he'd never been in trouble, he would only get probation. He also knew that from that day on he would ride clean. He had a child on the way, and he wanted to be there when it was born.

No sooner than the lawyer left, the two men got to visit with their women. Tracey was excited to hear that Meek would be coming home and hoped that they would never have to go through such a scare again. They had a child coming and Tracey definitely didn't want to be a single mother. On the other hand, Ashley was saddened by the news of Nahvi having to go back to prison. For some reason, they just couldn't catch a break. She loved him with all she had inside so she knew that him going to prison wouldn't change that.

"I'm so sorry, Ash. I keep fucking up and I don't blame you if you want to walk away and do your own thing. You deserve to be happy and yet, I keep hurting you."

"Oh Nahvi, I am happy and yeah, you've hurt me, but I have forgiven you and I already have what I deserve and that's you baby. I don't need anything else. We will work through this like we have everything else that's stood in our way. I love you and I'm not going anywhere."

Nahvi was glad to hear what Ashley had said. He had to have been doing something right for someone so beautiful and so real to love him and stick by him through it all.

The lawyer had worked it out so that Nahvi could go home for thirty days. He would wait to be sentenced. He made sure to stay out of the streets so he could get every minute he could with Ashley. Their love making became even more intense and they made sure to do it every day. Nahvi wanted to make sure he had his pussy fix ahead of time.

Meek threw him a party the weekend before he had to turn himself in for sentencing and his whole crew turned up to celebrate. He felt like the crew would ride with him this time because Meek would cast out anyone who didn't have his back.

"Yo Nahvi, my brotha. You know this shit ain't gonna be the same without you here."

"Preciate that, Meek. I ain't gonna lie. I love this shit but dawg when I get out this time I gotta go straight legit. Maybe I'll open up my own business or something."

Meek nodded because he liked the idea of what Nahvi said. "That shit sounds sweet but what kind of business would you want? Don't you gotta have some kind of skills other than slangin' to run a business?"

The two men shared a laugh because Meek had damn sure told the truth but although, all Nahvi knew was slangin' dope, he was a smart nigga, and he could do anything he set his mind to. Nahvi had a special surprise, and the party was winding down, so he wanted to propose a toast before anybody left. He stood and got the crowd's attention and then proceeded. "Hey, I want to thank everyone for coming out and participating. This really means a lot to me, but I want to talk about something that means more." He held out his hand to Ashley and she walked over to him and grabbed it. When she did, he dropped to one knee. "Ashley, I know that we have been through some shit together and still we managed to stay strong. There's no way I'd still be here if it wasn't for you and your love for me. I want to tell you how much I appreciate you and ask if you would give me the honor of being my wife. Will you marry me?"

Ashley couldn't help the tears of joy that formed in her eyes. She loved Nahvi so much and there was no way she would turn him down. "Yes Nahvi, yes I will marry you."

The day before Nahvi had to turn himself in, they got married in a small ceremony. He didn't want to wait until he was released, and Ashely didn't want to wait to carry his last name. After the two exchanged vows, Ashley had a surprise of her own to give him. When she handed him the small box he wondered what it could be and when he opened it, he found a positive pregnancy test.

"Does this mean?"

"Yes Nahvi, you're going to be a father."

Nahvi lifted her up in his arms and cried. He just couldn't believe his luck. He had totally been blessed and couldn't wait to get back home to his wife and seed. That night, him and Ashley made love for the last time until his days behind the wall were over.

The next day, her, Meek and Tracey drove him to the courthouse where he would be sentenced to three years.

Corey Robinson

Chapter Twenty Nine

"Welcome back, Karter. Didn't take you long to come back, and to think I almost put my money on you staying free."

Nahvi didn't find the comment that the correctional officer made funny at all. He had heard stories about the officers making bets on the inmates they thought would return, and the pot seemed to be pretty large. Nahvi hated being one of those inmates, but shit happened and there he was. He hated another muthafucka looking up his asshole as he bent over and spread his ass cheeks, but he knew that it was part of the process, and it didn't make him any less of a man.

He knew that he'd suffer the same bullshit every time he left from a visit, but it was something he was prepared to do as long as he could see his wife. He smiled at the thought of calling Ashley that every time he said it. When Nahvi was taken to his cell block, he ended up being housed with an older gangsta that went by the name of Ace.

Ace was in the pen for possession of cocaine and Nahvi wondered why a man of his age was still out there slangin' those packs. He should have been home being somebody's grandpa instead of sleeping under Nahvi. Ace had to be pushing sixty, but you couldn't tell it just by looking at him because he was fit and had very little gray. The guard had told Nahvi he was around that age and that everyone in the cell block referred to him as Pops. Ace was well respected in and out of the pen and Nahvi knew that they would get along just fine.

"What's up, old timer? Shouldn't your ass be out there taking your grandkids shopping or something instead of in here sleeping under me?"

Ace looked up at Nahvi and laughed but answered his question anyway. "Don't worry about my grandkids because although I'm in here, they still out there enjoying my money because even though I'm in here sleeping under you, my paper is still out there rolling. This is just a little vacation for me. What about you?"

Nahvi raised his eyebrows because he knew then that his new cell mate was a boss. He liked the sound of that. "Got charged with a burner and caught three straight."

"Yeah, well it happens to the best of us. Especially, when we choose the streets over everything else."

The comment pissed Nahvi off because the old man didn't know shit about him or what he had chosen. "Man, you don't know me and I ain't choose the streets over shit."

"Really, well Mr. JaNahvi Karter I may not know you personally, but I do know you and don't get so offensive. I know how those streets and the things it has to offer can blind you. That fast money is hard as hell to walk away from but you got to search deep and find the strength to do it or you'll end up in here like me. I'm going to die in here because I chose the streets. Don't make the same mistake. Now if you'll excuse me, I'm going to step out and let you get comfortable."

The words that the old man spoke brought chills to Nahvi. It was like Ace knew that he had been struggling with leaving the only thing he knew. The streets had a strong hold on him, and it was like he was in a tug of war. He loved Ashley but he also loved the adrenaline rush that he could only find on the block. No sooner than Nahvi got his shit situated, Ace walked back in the cell. "How's it going for you, young man? Did you think about what I said?"

Nahvi looked at him funny because he wanted to know why the man was so concerned. "You know what? Let me ask you this, why the hell are you so concerned with what I choose? What I do ain't gonna affect you so why do you care?"

Ace stared at Nahvi for a couple of minutes and then gave him the shock of his life. "Nahvi, I know that this may come as a shock to you but I'm your father."

"Man, get the fuck outta here. I don't know what the hell you up to, but you got the wrong muthafucka. Miss me with that bullshit."

Ace went to his locker and pulled out a photo and after he stared at it for a couple of minutes he passed it to Nahvi, who snatched it from his hand and asked.

"Man, what the fuck is this? The hell is this picture gonna prove?" Once Nahvi took the time to look at the picture in his hand, he felt like he was going to faint. It was a picture of his mother holding him in her arms. He had to be around two years old in the photo and he wondered where the old man had gotten it. "How the hell you get this picture?"

"Your momma sent it to me when you was about two and a half years old, and every year after that she sent me one up until the day she died." Ace handed Nahvi a stack of pictures and all of them were of him growing up. The last photo was from when he was fourteen, the age he was when she died. Once Ace saw that it had finally absorbed in Nahvi's mind, he handed him a stack of letters that were addressed in his mother's handwriting and then Ace walked out of the room again.

Nahvi sat down on the steel bench and began to read his mother's words. He couldn't believe that she had led him to think that his father didn't want him. The words on the pages were very clear that it was her own fault that Nahvi never knew his dad. How could she have been so cruel to let him believe that? Now that she was gone, he would never get the chance to ask her, but he hoped that Ace could give him the closure he needed.

As soon as Ace came back in the room, Nahvi questioned him. "Why wasn't you ever a part of my life? Why didn't you reach out to me? How come you made my mother raise me alone?"

Ace went in his locker and pulled out a small box and passed it to Nahvi and when he opened it, his heart broke even more. He found hundreds of cards and letters addressed to him that had been returned by his mother. "Why would she send them back to you? I don't understand."

"Well son when I met your mother she knew that I was heavy in the streets. I was only twenty four and your mom was the finest sixteen year old I had ever seen. I knew I could have gotten in trouble but there was no way I could resist her. I had a lady at the time and two children, but your momma said she only wanted to have fun and wasn't trying to cause me any drama but when she ended up pregnant with you, she wanted me to leave my family behind and be with her. I told her that we could still be together and that I had no problem taking care of my seed, but she wanted to move in with me. Of course, I couldn't let that happen because I already had my family there. Your momma wouldn't take no for an answer so she packed up her stuff and left her grandmother's house. She showed up on my front step, big belly and all and told my woman everything."

Ace paused to take a breath and then continued, "My woman took the kids and moved out and then put the cops on me and my operation. She knew that I had been being watched by the police, so she gave them enough evidence to send me away for forty straight years. I got about five left but I'm not sure I'll make it that long."

"So you been in here my whole life, and I never knew it. God, I'm so sorry."

"Nah, JaNahvi, don't be sorry because it's not your fault and I ain't even mad at your mother anymore. She was just a young girl in love. She never wanted you to be a product of the streets like I was. That's why she didn't want me in your life after I got popped with the drugs, but you was born with that shit in your veins and no matter what she did to prevent it, you was going to grow up and be a hustler. But I know that in your heart, you want out of them streets and they just keep calling you back over and over. You going to have to weigh your priorities and find out what's more important to you and then decide."

Nahvi had never known what it would be like to have a father but now that he had met his real dad, he didn't want to live another day without one. The two men spent the rest of the evening getting to know each other better and Nahvi was amazed at how much like him he really was. He shared his joy of knowing that the woman he loved would be having his child and even had it arranged so that Ashley could visit with both of them once a month. Nahvi was in a horrible predicament but shit actually started to look up for him. Things were going so good that he knew somewhere something bad would emerge.

"Hey baby, how are you and my son holding up?" Nahvi asked Ashely as he bent down to kiss her before their weekly visit. Six months had passed by so quickly and they both prayed that the other two and a half years went by just as quick.

"Why ain't Meek come with you this time. I wanna see my niece. I bet he spoils the hell out of her little ass." Meek and Tracey's daughter, Trameeka had been born only two weeks earlier and Nahvi couldn't wait to meet her. Meek had promised that he'd come with Ashley that weekend to visit and bring Meeka with him, but he was a no show. He didn't like the look on Ashley's face, and it made him feel like something was wrong. "Baby, why you so quiet? Everything aiight out there?"

Ashley bit her bottom lip and then told Nahvi everything. "I'm sorry, Nahvi, but Meek is dead."

Nahvi scrunched his eyebrows because he couldn't believe what Ashley had just told him. "The fuck did you just say?"

"Meek had set up a meeting with that dude y'all messed with in Austell but when he got there, the dude had another man with him that wanted more for less and when Meek turned him down, he shot him. Meek was able to get back in his truck and make it home to Tracey and the baby but before he could make it up the steps, he fell over. Tracey ran outside and he was able to tell her what happened but before he could tell he loved her, he took his last breath. I'm sorry, Nahvi."

"I told his ass that something wasn't right with that nigga. I can't believe he went back there anyway. I'm a kill that muthafucka when I get out of here. Man, that was my brotha and I gotta avenge him."

"And then what, Nahvi? Huh? Fuck me and your son right. Why can't you just let that shit go? Meek knew the consequences of street life the same as you. There's three ways out, Nahvi, and that's prison, death or by choice. Well Meek died by the gun and you're in prison because of the gun, you got to choose what means more to you, me and your son or the streets because when you come home, I will not sit around at night and worry about you coming home. Your son is going to need you, Nahvi and if I lose you to those streets, I won't have the heart to tell him that they meant more to you than him. I hate that Meek is gone too and all I can do is be there for my friend. Avenging his murder won't bring him back."

"Yeah, you right but if the shoe was on the other foot he'd kill a muthafucka for me."

"Nahvi, your father just came into your life. Don't make him mourn you. Meek will understand if you don't kill someone in his honor. When I told you that I'd stick by you no matter what, I meant it, but I won't stand by and let my son be a product." Ashley stood to leave and when Nahvi reached his hand out to stop her, she slapped it away. "Call me when you start thinking about me and the baby and can leave that street shit where it's at. I love you, Nahvi."

He couldn't believe that she had just walked out and left him standing there. He knew that she was upset because he promised her that he would never return to the streets and now he was talking about killing someone. Someone had to avenge his friend and who better to do it than him. The officer came up behind him and told him to return to his cell. He left and when he walked in the room his first tear drop fell.

Ace had a way of knowing about everything before anyone else, so he already knew why Nahvi was crying. He had been in that same piston before so he could feel his pain. "You know son, we all know that when we sign up for the kind of life we want to lead. There are consequences to our decisions. When you're in the drug game, you know that no night is promised to you, and one could end up being your last. We all understand that and yet we still go out there as if we are untouchable, but son, none of us really are. You got more to think about now. You have a wife who loves you and a son who is going to need his father. I want you to go out there and give my grandson all that I couldn't give you."

Nahvi understood what his pops was saying but it didn't ease the pain of his broken heart. Meek had been like a brother to him, and he had his back when no one else did. He didn't know how he would feel when he got out and Meek wasn't there. He could only imagine the pain that Tracey was feeling. Meek had only gotten a little time with his daughter and now she had to grow up without him. He needed to make sure that he was there for his son. He knew that Meek would understand. Nahvi had never been a praying man, but he sent one up to his creator anyway. "Yo God, I will never understand why you choose to take the ones you do but all I ask is that you take care of him. Tell Meek I'll make sure his girl and his seed are straight. Thanks."

Nahvi decided to wait until the next day to call Ashley and apologize. His mind was tired, and heart was heavy, so he knew that he needed some rest. As soon as his head hit the pillow, he was out. The next morning he woke up and took a shower and cried some more for his fallen soldier. His pops woke him up with a joint. "Where the hell you get this from?"

Ace smiled and took another pull, "When you go home, I want you to ask people about Ace. You'll find out that I'ma man of many means." He then pulled out a big manilla envelope and passed it to Nahvi.

"What's this? Some more surprises."

"Just open it," Ace said with a smile."

Nahvi did as he said and was shocked at what he saw. "Ever since the day you were born I been putting money in that account. I tried several times to give your momma some money for you, but she was so bitter about everything that she wouldn't accept a dime. So even after I got locked up I deposited money. When you go home, you go to that bank, and you give them the password and all that money will be given to you."

Nahvi looked at the amount and almost shit on himself, "Pops, this is eighty five million dollars. How did you?"

Ace cut him off. "It doesn't matter how. All that matters is that it is legal money, and it should be another reason to keep you off the streets. It's yours, son."

"Damn. Ashley ain't even going to believe this shit. I got to go call her. Thanks, pop."

Nahvi rushed out of the room and called his wife so he could give her the good news. He knew for sure that he would never have to go out in the streets again. He would be able to take care of his family forever and that shit felt good to him.

Ashley forgave her man and promised to go see him the next weekend but as always, drama would try to interfere with what they were building. A drama that would be hard to get rid of.

Corey Robinson

Chapter Thirty

Ashley was getting ready to go visit Nahvi when she heard her doorbell ring. She knew that it wasn't Tracey because she had went to stay a few weeks with Meek's grandmother so she wondered who it could have been.

When she opened the door she saw Tonya standing there with Kelvin's son and a new baby in her arms.

"I wanna go see Nahvi with you. He needs to spend time with his daughter."

"His daughter. What the hell are you talking about?"

"Uh, well, I know you remember what happened between me and him. I ended up pregnant and we had a daughter so I'm a need him to step up and take care of his. You understand, right?"

Ashley couldn't believe that another curve ball had been thrown to try and steal her happiness, but the last thing she would do is let Tonya know that she was an issue. "Okay, well I'm about to go visit him if you'd like to come. I'm sure if he has a child, he'd like to get to know them."

"So you're just going to accept this and let me go with you that easy. You're not even going to put up a fight?"

"Why should I? Nahvi is my husband and you or your daughter are not a threat to me."

Ashley walked out the door and locked it and went to get in her car. Tonya stood and watched her. She couldn't believe that Ashley had given in so easily. That wasn't her plan because Tonya wanted Nahvi for herself, and she would use anything she could to get him. Tonya finally grabbed Kelvin Junior's hand and pulled him like a rag doll to Ashley's car. She couldn't wait until Nahvi saw her walk in that visiting room. She planned on playing her position very well but

Nahvi was a smart nigga so she hoped her planned didn't backfire.

Nahvi sat at the regular table that him and Ashley used and when he saw her his heart skipped. Every time felt like the very first time she took his breath away, but when he looked closer and saw Tonya, he wanted to know what was going on. She had Kelvin Junior and another baby in her arms. The baby only looked to be a few months old, and he had a feeling of why she had brought the child. When they got close enough, he hugged Ashley and pulled her in for a kiss.

"Hello Nahvi, um as you can see, I brought company this time. It seems that Tonya has something to tell you so why don't we get that out of the way."

Ashley looked at Tonya and raised her eyebrows. She couldn't wait to hear Nahvi's reaction to what she was going to tell him.

"Hi Nahvi, I asked to come and see you because I wanted you to meet your daughter."

Nahvi looked at Tonya like he wanted to strangle her and then looked at the baby she held in her arms. "The fuck is you talking about Tonya? That ain't my child."

"Really, Nahvi? That pill you and your boy shoved into my veins didn't work. She belongs to you. I can't believe you're going to stand there and deny her like that."

About that time, another voice came from behind them.

"Hey son, what's going on here?"

Tonya didn't know who the man was, nor did she hear when Ashley asked to visit with both Nahvi and his dad. A privilege she got just from being Ace's daughter in law. His name carried plenty of weight in the pen and he was able to extend that to his son. He was going to stand in the background and not say anything but when he noticed the baby the other woman held, he knew that he had to step up.

"Who the hell are you?" Tonya asked with a scowl on her face.

"I'm Ace, Nahvi's father and just who might you be?"

"His father? Well that's funny because I have never heard him mention you. I'm Tonya and this is his daughter, Nahla."

Ace stepped a little closer so he could see the child and smiled a sarcastic smile, "Yeah, well it's funny that he's never mentioned you either. Do you mind if I hold her for a second?" He held out his arms so he could take the baby and Tonya hesitated at first but eventually passed her over. Ace looked closely at the child and then passed her back to her mother. "This little girl doesn't belong to my son."

"Uh, I think I know who my child's father is. I don't need you to tell me. I mean, she looks just like him."

"Nah, she don't look anything like him. She don't have Karter blood running through her veins and you dead ass wrong for coming up here and disrespecting my son and his wife like that. I suggest you turn around and walk out now. A bus runs through here in about twenty minutes. I suggest you catch it."

Tonya was so embarrassed and looked to Nahvi to help her out. "So, you're not going to say anything? You're just gonna stand there and entertain your bitch and not even acknowledge your daughter or me?"

Nahvi hadn't been paying Tonya or the child any attention because if his father said the baby wasn't his, then it wasn't, and he was not up to playing Tonya's little games. Nahvi looked at the little girl and felt no type of connection. He knew that Tonya was trying to cause friction in his relationship, but he refused to let her because he didn't want Ashley to be stressed while she carried her son. "Look Tonya, how bout I make a deal with you? My pops here is going to get the nurse to come take a DNA sample of that baby and if she turns out not to be mine then you take your ass outta here and never fuck with me or her again, but if she ends up being mine, I'll step up and make sure she's well taken care of. Pops, go head and get the nurse so we can get this shit over with because it's interfering with the time I need to spend with my wife and son."

Ace turned to go get the nurse, but Tonya stopped him.

"You know what? Don't even worry about it because my daughter is probably better off without you anyway."

She then turned and stormed out of the visitation room slowly dragging Kelvin Junior behind her. In a way, Nahvi felt bad for Tonya, but she brought all of her heartache on herself. He couldn't believe that she actually thought he'd let her pin a baby on him without proof. Him, Ashley, and Ace finally sat down so they could enjoy the visit. Nahvi had told Ashley to make that weekend their last visit until after their son was born. He didn't want her to keep taking the trips, but he knew that she was stubborn.

"Come on, Nahvi, I'm fine and so is he. This is your son I'm carrying, and he is just as hard headed as you. He enjoys these trips to see you and I'm not sure if I could stay away."

"Look Ash, I need you to stay home so I don't sit in here and worry. That lil muthafucka will be coming into the world in a few weeks and I need to make sure him and you are safe. You can come back after that, and hopefully you won't run into any more bullshit before then."

The two lovers shared a laugh because they knew that drama followed them everywhere they went. However, no matter how deep the drama pushed them they still ended up being on top. Only real love could survive what they had been through.

The visit flew by and when it was over, Ashley and Nahvi said their goodbyes. Ace had only stayed for a little of it because he knew they needed all the time they could get. The next time Ashley would come for a visit she'd be bringing his grandson and he couldn't wait. Ace had always prayed that he would meet his son one day and when the guard told him that Nahvi had been arrested and would be coming to the same prison, he arranged for them to be cellmates. He thought it would have been hard for Nahvi to accept him, but he welcomed him with open arms.

He'd had a man on the streets watching his son's every move. He'd told him not to interfere in his life unless he was in danger. He knew that Nahvi had to learn to grow up without a father because he couldn't be there and thought that maybe it was best if he continued to believe that his father had dipped out but when Nahvi finally fell in his lap he took that as a sign. Ace sat and waited for his son to come back from the visit and then he gave him some OG street knowledge.

"Son, why don't you sit down for a minute so I can spit some sense your way. I need to make sure that shit that happened out there doesn't happen again. You got a good strong woman in your life. Don't fuck it up like I did."

"Man, pops. I don't know why Tonya felt like she could try me like that. The fuck is wrong with her?"

"I'll tell you what's wrong with her," Ace pointed to Nahvi's crotch and continued, "That little head down there is what's wrong. Son, you made her act like that when you laid down with her. You gave her a reason to disrespect her first. You shouldn't have even been in a position for that to happen but since you were, you should be mad at yourself. That's the same thing your momma did when she had you but one look at you and I knew you had Karter blood, but that little girl didn't have one ounce."

"So, how could you tell that just by holding her. How you know she wasn't mine?"

"The first day I held you I could connect with your little spirit. The same way I did with my other two children but when I held that baby, there was no kind of connection at all. I'm telling you son, a man knows."

The room got quiet for a minute while both men sat deep in thought and Nahvi was the first one to break the silence, "So, where's your other two children? I'd like to meet them if I could."

The look on Ace's face answered Nahvi's question before his father had a chance to speak, "Well, you know that with street fame you don't only make lots of money, you also make lots of enemies too. I had more than I could even keep track of. People that smiled in my face ended up stabbing me in the back, but it was to be expected even though I paid them very well. I was never a greedy man and shared my street cred with everybody. I guess I ended up pissing the competition off and when they couldn't get to me, they got my wife and kids instead. They didn't know about you and because of that, I was able to keep you and your mother safe. So, sacrificing a relationship with you actually saved your life."

"Damn, I'm sorry to hear that I'll never be able to meet them, but I guess I also have a lot to be thankful for."

"Yeah son, and so do I. But remember, never fuck a bitch that you don't want nothing to do with or you'll face the consequences you did today. Be thankful you got a good woman because they are very hard to come by."

"Yeah, I guess I just got lucky. I'm tired though, so I'm about to lay my ass down. I love you pops and getting that gun charge was well worth it."

Nahvi hugged his father and jumped up in his bed not knowing that it would be his last night with him. When he woke up the next morning, he noticed that Ace had already gotten up and left the room, so he got out of bed and prepared himself for the day. When he was finished, his father still hadn't returned so he went on a search for him. Several other inmates that he had never talked to walked up to him and gave their condolences, but Nahvi had no idea why until he stepped to the guard on duty.

"Aye yo, Mr. Preston, you seen my pops around anywhere. I can't find him."

Mr. Preston gave him a somber look and guided him out into the hall. "I'm sorry, Mr. Karter but your father passed peacefully in his sleep in the middle of the night."

"The fuck outta here with that bullshit man. Wasn't shit wrong with him. He was healthy as a mufucka so miss me with that bullshit you talking about."

"I'm sorry, Mr. Karter. Maybe you should go talk to the warden. Him and your father were very good friends. He will be able to tell you more. Sorry for your loss."

Nahvi didn't want to believe what Mr. Preston had told him but his heart could tell that something was wrong. He felt empty inside because he had just got his father in his life only to lose him so soon. Ace had never seemed to be sick or anything else, so Nahvi needed some answers. When he walked in the warden's office he didn't waste any time. "What the hell happened to my father? There wasn't shit wrong with him so I'm a need you to tell me what's up with that?"

The warden was a tall white man with small beady eyes that looked sincere enough. He walked over to where Nahvi stood and told him everything he needed to know, "Mr. Karter, your father and I were very good friends. Have been for a long time. I don't know of any other man on earth that I respected more than him, but he was also a fighter. Ace has had Lung Cancer for a while now. It had already began to spread to other organs, but he refused to let it take him until he could make you a part of his life. You were all he was living for and now that y'all have made peace and he sees that you'll be okay, he was able to move on and rest in peace. For many, many years you were all he talks about. Ace was a good man, and you should be very proud to call him your father."

Nahvi sat down in the only other chair he saw and bawled like a child. His momma had always told him to never be afraid to let someone see you cry because it showed them that you were a real man. After he shed his share of tears, he got up to leave but before he walked out, the warden stopped him and told him something that would surely make him feel better. "Mr. Karter, your father knew that his time was about to end so he made arrangements for you."

"What kind of arrangements are you talking about? Stop hesitating and just tell me what's going on."

"You'll be getting released early. Actually, in only a couple of weeks. He wanted to make sure that you were present for the birth of your son. The paperwork is being taken care of as we speak, and once you leave, please make sure you never come back. Do what you need to do in order to stay out of here. So you can be there for your wife and kid. That's what your father asks of you."

"Yeah, I got it and I give you my word. This is it for me. I'm a be a son that makes his father proud. Thanks for looking out, man."

That night when Nahvi called Ashley, they shed tears together and made their bond even stronger. He didn't tell her that he'd be home for his son's birth because he wanted to keep it a surprise. He knew that once he held his first born his life would forever be changed. Nahvi was a street nigga but for Ashley and his son, he'd leave it all alone no matter how loud the streets called him.

Chapter Thirty One

Ashley felt the first contraction while she was getting out of bed, "Aaah shit. Oh my God, I need Nahvi here."

She knew that there was no way she could drive herself to the hospital, so she called for an ambulance. Once she got there, the room had already been set up for her to bring the new life into the world. As soon as the doctor walked in with the epidural, Ashley spoke up. "No, I want to do this natural. I want to feel the pain before my son takes it away with joy. He will be well worth it."

"Are you sure you don't want to reconsider, Mrs. Karter?"

When Ashley heard Nahvi's voice, she wanted to jump off the table and grab him. She couldn't believe that he was there and how he got there didn't matter as long as he was by her side.

"Oh my God, Nahvi. Baby, I don't even want to know. I'm just so happy you're here with me. I hope you're ready to meet your son."

About that time another contraction hit her hard and when the doctor checked her, he nodded. "Come on, let's get this little fella outta there."

Ashley held Nahvi's hand so tight, he thought she would break it. He had never been present during a woman giving birth so the experience he was sharing with the woman he loved was one that he'd never forget. The harder Ashley pushed, the more she cursed his soul. Finally, one last push brought them what they had been waiting for. They both cried when they laid eyes on their son and Ashley decided to let Nahvi name him, Jarell Ahmeek Karter after his father and best friend. It was a way for him to keep their memory alive.

Ashley watched Nahvi as he stared down at the baby in her arms and then she held him up for Nahvi to take. At first, he was hesitant because he had never held something so small and so fragile, but when he finally took him in his arms, he instantly fell in love. He knew right then that he would give his last heartbeat to protect the little guy he held in his arms. Ashley had truly given him the greatest gift and changed his life forever.

Nahvi had been given a phone when he was released and pulled it out of his pocket. "Here, take some flicks of me and my little gangsta."

"Now that's where you're wrong at because he is definitely not going to be a gangster," Ashley shared a laugh with Nahvi because they both knew that they would do their best to keep their son from being a product of the streets but no matter what he chose, they would love and support him completely.

Ashley and Ahmeek were released from the hospital two days later and Nahvi couldn't wait to get them home where they could begin their life together as a family. They had been through hell and back and still managed to come out on top. Nahvi enjoyed his nights at home with his wife and son, but he was itching to hit the block. Ashley could see the desire deep in his eyes because she had learned him so well. Nahvi didn't need the hustle because not only did he have stacks upon stacks, but his pop's millions put him beyond where he thought he would be, but he wanted the streets. It was familiar and comfortable to him because the streets had been good to him all of his life.

"I see it in your eyes, Nahvi and I want you to know that as bad as I want you to stay home with us, I will stand by you no matter what your decision is. My love for you will never fade so you never have to worry about that."

Nahvi knew that Ashley was sincere but what would happen to her and his seed if he ended up like Meek? Was he willing to put all their futures in jeopardy for another night in the streets?

"It's okay baby I understand. If you need to go out there and get it out of your system, then go. I know that the streets is all you've known and I want you to be happy. We'll be here waiting for you to come back."

Nahvi couldn't believe what Ashley had said. He felt bad about wanting to go out there, but she was right. He had to get it out of his system. He stood up and kissed Ashley and his seed on the forehead and then walked out of their home to go to more familiar surroundings. He first went to one of his and Meek's old trap houses. He knew that while he was locked up, things didn't pause. They only continued to move. All the same workers were there and a couple he had never seen and while they were all glad to see him, the shit just didn't feel the same anymore.

"Sup, Nahvi? Nigga, I don't understand how you made it out of that shit hole still sane. What's good with you, playa?" One of the top workers asked while giving him some dap.

"You the one that seems to be good my nigga. Looks like you holding shit down pretty damn good."

"Yeah man, somebody had to take control. I mean, you were locked up and Meek, well you know. Shit was just fucked up so I stepped up to the plate but you back now dawg and I can step back down. Things sure ain't the same out here without you and ya boy. You coming back?

Nahvi thought about the question and then thought about all he had gained. He had everything he ever wanted. Money, cars, a nice home, a good woman, and a shorty to carry on his legacy. He couldn't even lie; he didn't think that coming back out in the streets would be a good idea.

"Nah man, you got it. I got other priorities now so I'm a let you keep this out here. It's been good."

Nahvi's best man was gone and no matter who he chose to ride beside him they could never take Meek's spot. He took the good memories and the bad ones and got back in his ride. The streets just wasn't the place for him anymore. So, he started his money green Denali and took his ass home to be with the love he found in the trenches.

To Be Continued...
Love in the Trenches 2
Coming Soon

Lock Down Publications and Ca$h Presents
assisted publishing packages.

BASIC PACKAGE $499
Editing
Cover Design
Formatting

UPGRADED PACKAGE $800
Typing
Editing
Cover Design
Formatting

ADVANCE PACKAGE $1,200
Typing
Editing
Cover Design
Formatting
Copyright registration
Proofreading
Upload book to Amazon

LDP SUPREME PACKAGE $1,500
Typing
Editing
Cover Design
Formatting
Copyright registration
Proofreading

Corey Robinson

Set up Amazon account
Upload book to Amazon
Advertise on LDP Amazon and Facebook page

***Other services available upon request.
Additional charges may apply
Lock Down Publications
P.O. Box 944
Stockbridge, GA 30281-9998
Phone # 470 303-9761

Submission Guideline

Submit the first three chapters of your completed manuscript to ldpsubmissions@gmail.com, subject line: Your book's title. The manuscript must be in a .doc file and sent as an attachment. Document should be in Times New Roman, double spaced and in size 12 font. Also, provide your synopsis and full contact information. If sending multiple submissions, they must each be in a separate email.

Have a story but no way to send it electronically? You can still submit to LDP/Ca$h Presents. Send in the first three chapters, written or typed, of your completed manuscript to:

LDP: Submissions Dept
Po Box 944
Stockbridge, Ga 30281

DO NOT send original manuscript. Must be a duplicate.

Provide your synopsis and a cover letter containing your full contact information.

Thanks for considering LDP and Ca$h Presents.

Corey Robinson

NEW RELEASES

A GANGSTA'S PAIN 3 by J-BLUNT

THE STREETS NEVER LET GO 3 by ROBERT
BAPTISTE

BODYMORE KINGPINS by ROMELL TUKES

LOVE IN THE TRENCHES by COREY ROBINSON

Coming Soon from Lock Down Publications/Ca$h Presents

BLOOD OF A BOSS **VI**

SHADOWS OF THE GAME II

TRAP BASTARD II

By **Askari**

LOYAL TO THE GAME **IV**

By **T.J. & Jelissa**

TRUE SAVAGE **VIII**

MIDNIGHT CARTEL IV

DOPE BOY MAGIC IV

CITY OF KINGZ III

NIGHTMARE ON SILENT AVE II

THE PLUG OF LIL MEXICO II

CLASSIC CITY II

By **Chris Green**

BLAST FOR ME **III**

A SAVAGE DOPEBOY III

CUTTHROAT MAFIA III

DUFFLE BAG CARTEL VII

HEARTLESS GOON VI

By **Ghost**

A HUSTLER'S DECEIT III

KILL ZONE II

BAE BELONGS TO ME III

TIL DEATH II

By **Aryanna**

KING OF THE TRAP III

Corey Robinson

By **T.J. Edwards**
GORILLAZ IN THE BAY V
3X KRAZY III
STRAIGHT BEAST MODE III
De'Kari
KINGPIN KILLAZ IV
STREET KINGS III
PAID IN BLOOD III
CARTEL KILLAZ IV
DOPE GODS III
Hood Rich
SINS OF A HUSTLA II
ASAD
YAYO V
Bred In The Game 2
S. Allen
THE STREETS WILL TALK II
By Yolanda Moore
SON OF A DOPE FIEND III
HEAVEN GOT A GHETTO II
SKI MASK MONEY II
By Renta
LOYALTY AIN'T PROMISED III
By Keith Williams
I'M NOTHING WITHOUT HIS LOVE II
SINS OF A THUG II
TO THE THUG I LOVED BEFORE II

Love in the Trenches

IN A HUSTLER I TRUST II

By Monet Dragun

QUIET MONEY IV

EXTENDED CLIP III

THUG LIFE IV

By **Trai'Quan**

THE STREETS MADE ME IV

By **Larry D. Wright**

IF YOU CROSS ME ONCE III

ANGEL V

By **Anthony Fields**

THE STREETS WILL NEVER CLOSE IV

By K'ajji

HARD AND RUTHLESS III

KILLA KOUNTY IV

By Khufu

MONEY GAME III

By Smoove Dolla

JACK BOYS VS DOPE BOYS IV

A GANGSTA'S QUR'AN V

COKE GIRLZ II

COKE BOYS II

LIFE OF A SAVAGE V

CHI'RAQ GANGSTAS V

SOSA GANG II

BRONX SAVAGES II

BODYMORE KINGPINS II

Corey Robinson

By Romell Tukes

MURDA WAS THE CASE III

Elijah R. Freeman

AN UNFORESEEN LOVE IV

BABY, I'M WINTERTIME COLD III

By **Meesha**

QUEEN OF THE ZOO III

By **Black Migo**

CONFESSIONS OF A JACKBOY III

By Nicholas Lock

GRIMEY WAYS III

By Ray Vinci

KING KILLA II

By Vincent "Vitto" Holloway

BETRAYAL OF A THUG III

By Fre$h

THE MURDER QUEENS III

By Michael Gallon

THE BIRTH OF A GANGSTER III

By Delmont Player

TREAL LOVE II

By Le'Monica Jackson

FOR THE LOVE OF BLOOD III

By Jamel Mitchell

RAN OFF ON DA PLUG II

By Paper Boi Rari

Love in the Trenches

HOOD CONSIGLIERE III

By Keese

PRETTY GIRLS DO NASTY THINGS II

By Nicole Goosby

PROTÉGÉ OF A LEGEND III

LOVE IN THE TRENCHES II

By Corey Robinson

IT'S JUST ME AND YOU II

By Ah'Million

BORN IN THE GRAVE III

By Self Made Tay

FOREVER GANGSTA III

By Adrian Dulan

GORILLAZ IN THE TRENCHES II

By SayNoMore

THE COCAINE PRINCESS VII

By King Rio

CRIME BOSS II

Playa Ray

LOYALTY IS EVERYTHING III

Molotti

HERE TODAY GONE TOMORROW II

By Fly Rock

REAL G'S MOVE IN SILENCE II

By Von Diesel

Corey Robinson

Love in the Trenches

BLOODY COMMAS I & II

SKI MASK CARTEL I II & III

KING OF NEW YORK I II,III IV V

RISE TO POWER I II III

COKE KINGS I II III IV V

BORN HEARTLESS I II III IV

KING OF THE TRAP I II

By **T.J. Edwards**

IF LOVING HIM IS WRONG...I & II

LOVE ME EVEN WHEN IT HURTS I II III

By **Jelissa**

WHEN THE STREETS CLAP BACK I & II III

THE HEART OF A SAVAGE I II III IV

MONEY MAFIA I II

LOYAL TO THE SOIL I II III

By **Jibril Williams**

A DISTINGUISHED THUG STOLE MY HEART I II & III

LOVE SHOULDN'T HURT I II III IV

RENEGADE BOYS I II III IV

PAID IN KARMA I II III

SAVAGE STORMS I II III

AN UNFORESEEN LOVE I II III

BABY, I'M WINTERTIME COLD I II

By **Meesha**

A GANGSTER'S CODE I &, II III

A GANGSTER'S SYN I II III

THE SAVAGE LIFE I II III

Corey Robinson

CHAINED TO THE STREETS I II III
BLOOD ON THE MONEY I II III
A GANGSTA'S PAIN I II III
By J-Blunt
PUSH IT TO THE LIMIT
By **Bre' Hayes**
BLOOD OF A BOSS **I, II, III, IV, V**
SHADOWS OF THE GAME
TRAP BASTARD
By **Askari**
THE STREETS BLEED MURDER **I, II & III**
THE HEART OF A GANGSTA I II& III
By **Jerry Jackson**
CUM FOR ME I II III IV V VI VII VIII
An **LDP Erotica Collaboration**
BRIDE OF A HUSTLA **I II & II**
THE FETTI GIRLS **I, II& III**
CORRUPTED BY A GANGSTA I, II III, IV
BLINDED BY HIS LOVE
THE PRICE YOU PAY FOR LOVE I, II ,III
DOPE GIRL MAGIC I II III
By **Destiny Skai**
WHEN A GOOD GIRL GOES BAD
By **Adrienne**
THE COST OF LOYALTY I II III
By Kweli
A GANGSTER'S REVENGE **I II III & IV**

206

Love in the Trenches

THE BOSS MAN'S DAUGHTERS I II III IV V

A SAVAGE LOVE **I & II**

BAE BELONGS TO ME I II

A HUSTLER'S DECEIT I, II, III

WHAT BAD BITCHES DO I, II, III

SOUL OF A MONSTER I II III

KILL ZONE

A DOPE BOY'S QUEEN I II III

TIL DEATH

By **Aryanna**

A KINGPIN'S AMBITON

A KINGPIN'S AMBITION **II**

I MURDER FOR THE DOUGH

By **Ambitious**

TRUE SAVAGE I II III IV V VI VII

DOPE BOY MAGIC I, II, III

MIDNIGHT CARTEL I II III

CITY OF KINGZ I II

NIGHTMARE ON SILENT AVE

THE PLUG OF LIL MEXICO II

CLASSIC CITY

By **Chris Green**

A DOPEBOY'S PRAYER

By **Eddie "Wolf" Lee**

THE KING CARTEL **I, II & III**

By **Frank Gresham**

THESE NIGGAS AIN'T LOYAL **I, II & III**

Corey Robinson

By **Nikki Tee**
GANGSTA SHYT **I II &III**
By **CATO**
THE ULTIMATE BETRAYAL
By **Phoenix**
BOSS'N UP **I , II & III**
By **Royal Nicole**
I LOVE YOU TO DEATH
By **Destiny J**
I RIDE FOR MY HITTA
I STILL RIDE FOR MY HITTA
By **Misty Holt**
LOVE & CHASIN' PAPER
By **Qay Crockett**
TO DIE IN VAIN
SINS OF A HUSTLA
By **ASAD**
BROOKLYN HUSTLAZ
By **Boogsy Morina**
BROOKLYN ON LOCK I & II
By **Sonovia**
GANGSTA CITY
By **Teddy Duke**
A DRUG KING AND HIS DIAMOND I & II III
A DOPEMAN'S RICHES
HER MAN, MINE'S TOO I, II
CASH MONEY HO'S

Love in the Trenches

THE WIFEY I USED TO BE I II

PRETTY GIRLS DO NASTY THINGS

By Nicole Goosby

TRAPHOUSE KING **I II & III**

KINGPIN KILLAZ I II III

STREET KINGS I II

PAID IN BLOOD **I II**

CARTEL KILLAZ I II III

DOPE GODS I II

By **Hood Rich**

LIPSTICK KILLAH **I, II, III**

CRIME OF PASSION I II & III

FRIEND OR FOE I II III

By **Mimi**

STEADY MOBBN' **I, II, III**

THE STREETS STAINED MY SOUL I II III

By **Marcellus Allen**

WHO SHOT YA **I, II, III**

SON OF A DOPE FIEND I II

HEAVEN GOT A GHETTO

SKI MASK MONEY

Renta

GORILLAZ IN THE BAY **I II III IV**

TEARS OF A GANGSTA I II

3X KRAZY I II

STRAIGHT BEAST MODE I II

DE'KARI

Corey Robinson

TRIGGADALE I II III
MURDAROBER WAS THE CASE I II
Elijah R. Freeman
GOD BLESS THE TRAPPERS I, II, III
THESE SCANDALOUS STREETS I, II, III
FEAR MY GANGSTA I, II, III IV, V
THESE STREETS DON'T LOVE NOBODY I, II
BURY ME A G I, II, III, IV, V
A GANGSTA'S EMPIRE I, II, III, IV
THE DOPEMAN'S BODYGAURD I II
THE REALEST KILLAZ I II III
THE LAST OF THE OGS I II III
Tranay Adams
THE STREETS ARE CALLING
Duquie Wilson
MARRIED TO A BOSS I II III
By Destiny Skai & Chris Green
KINGZ OF THE GAME I II III IV V VI
CRIME BOSS
Playa Ray
SLAUGHTER GANG I II III
RUTHLESS HEART I II III
By Willie Slaughter
FUK SHYT
By Blakk Diamond
DON'T F#CK WITH MY HEART I II
By Linnea

Love in the Trenches

ADDICTED TO THE DRAMA I II III

IN THE ARM OF HIS BOSS II

By Jamila

YAYO I II III IV

A SHOOTER'S AMBITION I II

BRED IN THE GAME

By S. Allen

TRAP GOD I II III

RICH $AVAGE I II III

MONEY IN THE GRAVE I II III

By Martell Troublesome Bolden

FOREVER GANGSTA I II

GLOCKS ON SATIN SHEETS I II

By Adrian Dulan

TOE TAGZ I II III IV

LEVELS TO THIS SHYT I II

IT'S JUST ME AND YOU

By Ah'Million

KINGPIN DREAMS I II III

RAN OFF ON DA PLUG

By Paper Boi Rari

CONFESSIONS OF A GANGSTA I II III IV

CONFESSIONS OF A JACKBOY I II

By Nicholas Lock

I'M NOTHING WITHOUT HIS LOVE

SINS OF A THUG

TO THE THUG I LOVED BEFORE

Corey Robinson

A GANGSTA SAVED XMAS

IN A HUSTLER I TRUST

By Monet Dragun

CAUGHT UP IN THE LIFE I II III

THE STREETS NEVER LET GO I II III

By Robert Baptiste

NEW TO THE GAME I II III

MONEY, MURDER & MEMORIES I II III

By **Malik D. Rice**

LIFE OF A SAVAGE I II III IV

A GANGSTA'S QUR'AN I II III IV

MURDA SEASON I II III

GANGLAND CARTEL I II III

CHI'RAQ GANGSTAS I II III IV

KILLERS ON ELM STREET I II III

JACK BOYZ N DA BRONX I II III

A DOPEBOY'S DREAM I II III

JACK BOYS VS DOPE BOYS I II III

COKE GIRLZ

COKE BOYS

SOSA GANG

BRONX SAVAGES

BODYMORE KINGPINS

By Romell Tukes

LOYALTY AIN'T PROMISED I II

By Keith Williams

QUIET MONEY I II III

Love in the Trenches

THUG LIFE I II III

EXTENDED CLIP I II

A GANGSTA'S PARADISE

By **Trai'Quan**

THE STREETS MADE ME I II III

By **Larry D. Wright**

THE ULTIMATE SACRIFICE I, II, III, IV, V, VI

KHADIFI

IF YOU CROSS ME ONCE I II

ANGEL I II III IV

IN THE BLINK OF AN EYE

By **Anthony Fields**

THE LIFE OF A HOOD STAR

By **Ca$h & Rashia Wilson**

THE STREETS WILL NEVER CLOSE I II III

By **K'ajji**

CREAM I II III

THE STREETS WILL TALK

By **Yolanda Moore**

NIGHTMARES OF A HUSTLA I II III

By **King Dream**

CONCRETE KILLA I II III

VICIOUS LOYALTY I II III

By **Kingpen**

HARD AND RUTHLESS I II

MOB TOWN 251

THE BILLIONAIRE BENTLEYS I II III

Corey Robinson

REAL G'S MOVE IN SILENCE
By Von Diesel
GHOST MOB
Stilloan Robinson
MOB TIES I II III IV V VI
SOUL OF A HUSTLER, HEART OF A KILLER I II
GORILLAZ IN THE TRENCHES
By SayNoMore
BODYMORE MURDERLAND I II III
THE BIRTH OF A GANGSTER I II
By Delmont Player
FOR THE LOVE OF A BOSS
By C. D. Blue
MOBBED UP I II III IV
THE BRICK MAN I II III IV V
THE COCAINE PRINCESS I II III IV V VI
By King Rio
KILLA KOUNTY I II III IV
By Khufu
MONEY GAME I II
By Smoove Dolla
A GANGSTA'S KARMA I II III
By FLAME
KING OF THE TRENCHES I II III
by **GHOST & TRANAY ADAMS**
QUEEN OF THE ZOO I II
By **Black Migo**

Love in the Trenches

GRIMEY WAYS I II

By Ray Vinci

XMAS WITH AN ATL SHOOTER

By Ca$h & Destiny Skai

KING KILLA

By Vincent "Vitto" Holloway

BETRAYAL OF A THUG I II

By Fre$h

THE MURDER QUEENS I II

By Michael Gallon

TREAL LOVE

By Le'Monica Jackson

FOR THE LOVE OF BLOOD I II

By Jamel Mitchell

HOOD CONSIGLIERE I II

By Keese

PROTÉGÉ OF A LEGEND I II

LOVE IN THE TRENCHES

By Corey Robinson

BORN IN THE GRAVE I II

By Self Made Tay

MOAN IN MY MOUTH

By XTASY

TORN BETWEEN A GANGSTER AND A GENTLEMAN

By J-BLUNT & Miss Kim

LOYALTY IS EVERYTHING I II

Molotti

Corey Robinson

HERE TODAY GONE TOMORROW
By Fly Rock
PILLOW PRINCESS
By S. Hawkins

<u>BOOKS BY LDP'S CEO, CA$H</u>

TRUST IN NO MAN

TRUST IN NO MAN 2

TRUST IN NO MAN 3

BONDED BY BLOOD

SHORTY GOT A THUG

THUGS CRY

THUGS CRY 2

THUGS CRY 3

TRUST NO BITCH

TRUST NO BITCH 2

TRUST NO BITCH 3

TIL MY CASKET DROPS

RESTRAINING ORDER

RESTRAINING ORDER 2

IN LOVE WITH A CONVICT

LIFE OF A HOOD STAR

XMAS WITH AN ATL SHOOTER

Corey Robinson

Printed in the USA
CPSIA information can be obtained
at www.ICGtesting.com
LVHW010554271223
767470LV00003B/45

9 781958 111857